By Katharine E. Hamilton

ISBN-13: 978-1-7358125-2-6
ISBN- 13: 978-1-7358125-1-9

Mary & Bright

www.katharinehamilton.com

Cover Design by Kerry Prater.

Thank you to my momma and daddy, Kelly and Annetta Hamilton, for making sure each Christmas was filled with joy and magic.

Acknowledgments

My editor, Lauren Hanson. Adding another book to the ranks, Woo hoo!

My cover designer, Kerry Prater, for always coming through with beautiful work.

My beta reader team: Sherrill, Danielle, Megan D., Megan W., Macy, Sarah, and Carolyn. Thank you all for always being honest with your feedback and for being a part of Team Katharine.

And special thanks to my readers. You guys are the best. I count myself fortunate and completely lucky and blessed to have you on my side. Thank you!

« CHAPTER ONE »

Snow didn't bother her, nor did the cold or icy roads. The problem with the drive to her parents' home for the holidays was that she felt it a waste of time. There was no *holiday* in Mary Rutherford's Christmas holiday when it came to her parents. Her next three weeks would be spent helping her mother find the perfect dress, the perfect venue, and the perfect food for the annual Christmas party of Rutherford and Sons. Yes, *sons*. Her great-grandfather, the founding member of R&S Distribution had passed the throne of responsibility to Mary's grandfather. And upon his passing eleven years prior, the mantle then passed to her own father. Unfortunately for Rowan Rutherford, he only had a daughter. Mary. There'd be no continuation of the *Sons* after her father, and potentially not even to a Rutherford. No cousins worked within the company and Mary did not work for the company either, though not for lack of trying. Her father had refused to hire her on the premise that her talents and skills were best utilized elsewhere. He'd wanted her to venture out of the small town of Ransforth, to make something of herself without the stigma of being a Rutherford. Mary felt he just didn't want to face the fact that one day the chain of generational passage would eventually be broken, unless he went against tradition and passed it to his daughter. She wasn't upset about his decision anymore. She had been for years, but maturity, a life of her own, and a job she loved eased that disappointment until it no longer existed. She *did,* however, harbor some resentment when it came to the annual Christmas party. For her *not* to be an employee with the company, she sure did have to help her mother plan a stellar company soirée every year.

She turned down Main Street, the twinkling lights of Christmas window displays altering the local businesses into Santa's Wonderland, or so it seemed. December marked a complete transformation to the town of Ransforth and its inhabitants. Patience was granted, disputes placed on hold, and kindness seemed to infiltrate everyone during the holiday season. Mary loved it. It was one of the few things Mary loved about Ransforth. She sighed contentedly as she spotted Nonnie Smith's bakery up ahead. She pulled into a vacant parking spot and studied Nonnie's window display. Nonnie Smith had been a Ransforth staple since before Mary was even born. Known for her cookies, pies, and cakes, Nonnie's treats were reserved and her talents scheduled months and years in advance for Christmas parties. But not for the Rutherfords. Mary never knew why her mother didn't book Nonnie for R&S Distribution's Christmas party, but year after year, Molly Rutherford hired a new stiff-necked catering company. Their food was delectable, but not like Nonnie's. The Christmas tree in the window turned electronically, its ornaments hand-crafted by children of Ransforth for decades. Mary wasn't sure how Nonnie decided which ornaments graced the tree each year as she probably had thousands to choose from, but every December first, Nonnie's tree went up in the window, and children would race over after school to see if they were one of the lucky ones chosen. Mary remembered in second grade when her handcrafted Christmas unicorn made it near the top of the tree, just beneath the angel. A place of honor. She still felt a warmth in her chest when she thought about how proud she'd been. She'd walked home from school, eager to share her exciting news with her parents, only to find their own Christmas trees being decorated by the house staff in elegant hues of red and gold with ornaments Mary was never allowed to touch. All were impeccably designed for the annual Christmas party. The house took on a museum-type quality during the holiday season. Look, but don't touch. Be quiet, but be present. And "For heaven's sake, Mary, don't disturb the guests," she could hear her mother saying. She'd never felt at home in the grand mansion at the edge of town. Even now, as she sat staring at Nonnie's shop, an emptiness filled her. But her gloomy thoughts disappeared as Nonnie spotted her through the glass door and beamed. She waved excitedly at Mary and motioned for her to come inside the shop. Mary didn't even bother with her coat. Braving the few seconds of winter chill, she hopped out of her car and darted across the sidewalk to an awaiting Nonnie and a warm hug.

Nonnie rubbed her hands up and down Mary's arms. "You're going to freeze to death without a coat, Mary Rutherford," she scolded, though her tone was pleasant and her attention loving. She hugged Mary close once more and pulled back. "Now, let me have a look at you." Her eyes, as deep green as the Christmas tree that graced her window, sparkled. "Gorgeous, as always. A little too thin, but nothing I can't handle." She winked. "Come, let me get you some hot chocolate and your choice of cookie." She pointed to the display counter and Mary walked over, saliva already puddling in her mouth at the sight of such delicious creations. "Will it be the usual?" Nonnie asked, sliding a mug of cocoa over the counter and waiting expectantly for Mary to make her choice of cookie. Her usual, as Nonnie described her once-a-year purchase, was a simple gingerbread man cookie, iced with loving care and candy buttons.

"You know me too well, Nonnie. Yes, the usual." Mary pointed towards the gingerbread man and Nonnie retrieved it and placed it on a small white china plate.

"Do you have the time to sit a spell?" Nonnie motioned towards a small wooden table with two chairs that sat towards the front of the shop.

"I could spare a few minutes." Mary grinned and walked her treats over to the table while Nonnie helped herself to her own mug of hot chocolate. When the plump woman slid into her seat, she sighed, a happy satisfied gleam in her eye at the sight of Mary.

"How have you been, Mary?"

Every year Nonnie asked her the same question and every year, Mary was sure Nonnie knew she struggled with what to say. "I've been good. Busy mostly, with work."

"Still enjoying your consulting job? Oh, what company was it?"

"Donnings Footwear," Mary replied.

"That's right. You oversee distribution, correct?"

"I do. I'm a Rutherford, distribution is what we do." Nonnie smiled knowingly as the last of Mary's sentence was said with a touch of cynicism. "But how about you, Nonnie? I love your tree."

Proudly, Nonnie gazed over at her window display. "Thank you. It was hard to choose this year, so many sweet ornaments. But the children have already made the rounds to see which ones made it." She chuckled softly. "Sweet darlings." She took a sip of her cocoa. "Your parents preparing for their big party? I've heard several R&S employees commenting on it over the last several days."

"I guess. I haven't been home yet."

"I'm your first stop?" Nonnie straightened in her chair and gleamed. "I feel so special. I think that calls for two cookies." She hurried towards the counter and came back with a warm chocolate chip that she split with Mary.

"I spoke with Mom a week ago and they seemed to be floundering a bit with party preparations for some reason. She didn't say why, but it sounded as if my dad wasn't planning to help."

"It's a busy time of year, especially for R&S Distribution. I'm sure he is rather swamped with his work. But Rowan always pulls off the party of the century, so I'm sure it will come together." She patted Mary's hand, though both women knew Nonnie had no insight into the party. Though many townspeople were invited, Nonnie never made the guest list, no matter how badly Mary would have loved to have her there.

Mary swiped a hand through her long hair and settled back in her chair on an exhale. "Well, we'll see what the mood is when I step inside the house this evening. How are your grandkids?"

"Oh, they're absolutely wonderful! Paula is in D.C. working for a senator there. Grace still lives here with her family. She now has three little ones and a fourth on the way. Bless her heart, she's the size of one of the parade floats," Nonnie giggled. "And Brighten, well, he actually moved back to Ransforth about six months ago."

"Really?" Mary's brows rose at the mention of Nonnie's grandson moving back to town. She and Brighten had been a part of the same graduating class in high school. Though they hung out in two different crowds, Brighten Smith was always kind, just like his grandmother. "Wasn't he living out in California?"

"He was." Nonnie nodded. "He'd moved out there to be closer to his girlfriend."

"What made him decide to move back this way?" Mary asked, not caring if the question was too nosy. Nonnie lived to talk about her grandkids and their lives, and Brighten Smith was always a hot topic in town, whether he lived there or not.

"He missed me." She laughed at her own joke and Mary smirked as she took a sip of her cocoa. "But in all honesty, his relationship didn't last, he did not care for California, and since he can work from anywhere really with his graphic design business, he decided he wanted to be here with his family. I think Grace's children played a part in his decision as well. He loves spending time with them and being so far from them was hard on him."

"Well, I'm glad, for your sake and Grace's, that he decided to come back."

"When do *you* plan on moving back?" Nonnie asked and had Mary almost spitting out her drink.

"I don't think that will ever be in the cards for me," Mary admitted.

"And why not? Your Dad is getting close to retiring, isn't he? I figured you'd be prepping for his role at R&S."

"Unfortunately, that has never been a part of the family plan."

"Hogwash." Nonnie shook her head. "You're a Rutherford, and a Rutherford has always run R&S."

"You forget that it is Rutherford and *Sons*, Nonnie."

"And? So what? You're a bright mind and hard worker."

"I'm glad you think so." Mary squeezed her hand.

"And you work in distribution already. Why, Rowan would be a fool not to hand the company over to you. Besides, if he didn't, who would he choose to run it?"

"Your guess is as good as mine. Dad's never really expanded upon that topic with me."

"Well, for the town's sake, I hope it's you."

"Thanks, but I'm actually happy where I'm at. Donnings has been good to me over the years."

"But it's so far away." Nonnie semi-pouted before she broke into her familiar smile. "That's just me being selfish. I want you here all the time." That sentiment meant more to Mary than Nonnie would ever know. Her love over the years had given many a kid a feeling of importance. And though Mary belonged to one of the most important and influential families in town, she herself had never felt important. Her parents, though they had provided well for her over the years, were never the nurturing sort. She'd merely existed in their household. She'd had maids to do her bidding, a cook to feed her, a nanny to play with her, and a personal trainer to make sure she stayed fit and healthy. With so many people in Mary's personal life, where did her parents have a chance to fit in as well? She wasn't bitter about her upbringing; she just wasn't attached to it. Her best memories revolved around school and friends. She'd loved visiting friends at their houses. They were always so inviting and happy, especially when they were able to spend time together. Family meals were foreign to Mary, and she loved being a spectator to something so ordinary when she had the opportunity.

A Christmas tune chimed as the front door to the bakery opened and a man walked inside, rubbing his hands together to generate some warmth. He was tall, his dark hair covered with a beanie and his scarf pulled up around his face. As he unwrapped the scarf, Nonnie stood to her feet. "I'll get out of your hair," Mary whispered.

"Nonsense." Nonnie waved her back down. "It's just Bright."

Surprise lit Mary's face as she saw her old acquaintance unwind the scarf around his neck and remove his beanie and coat. "It's freezing out there, Nonnie. I sure hope these were worth it." He pulled a paper sack out of his coat pocket and handed it over to his grandmother.

"They are. I can't make reindeer cookies without these sugar balls for their jingle bells." She kissed him on the cheek and motioned towards Mary. "Look who stopped by to say hello."

Mary stood as Bright turned around, and she felt her knees jitter at the sight of his handsome face. This was definitely not the Brighten Smith she remembered from high school days. For one, he'd filled out his lanky, tall frame, but his eyes still held the same mischievous gleam and kindness they had growing up. His face did not register who she was.

"I'm sorry," He placed a hand over his chest. "but I can't seem to place you. Do we know each other?"

Mary grinned. She actually liked that people didn't recognize her from her high school years. Those days were best forgotten anyway. The braces, the frizzy hair, the awkward acne. She cringed at the thought. "Mary. Mary Rutherford."

His jaw dropped as his entire face lifted into a welcoming smile. "No way! Mary Rutherford, wow! You look fantastic." He swept her into a hug, the Smiths' usual greeting, before he set her to rights. "How've you been? Wow, how many years has it been since we've last seen each other?"

"Quite a few," Mary replied.

"Mary's here for the holidays and stopped by on her way to her parents' place. I was her first stop," Nonnie boasted proudly.

Bright took a step back and looked Mary up and down once more. "Wow, can't believe it. You're an adult now. It's crazy."

Mary laughed. "You too. I wouldn't have recognized you either if you hadn't smiled that cheeky smile of yours."

He laughed as he motioned towards the small table again and took Nonnie's seat, as his grandmother busied herself making him his own mug of cocoa and placed a small plate of ginger bites in front of them so they could catch up.

"So other than looking great, have you been great?" Bright asked, popping a cookie into his mouth.

Mary nodded. "I've been good."

"Where are you at these days?"

"Over in Landisburg."

"Do you get down here often to see your parents?"

"Just once a year around the holidays," Mary answered. "The annual Christmas party is a must." She tried to hide her annoyance by taking a sip of her cocoa. Nonnie always knew how to make the best cocoa, the chocolate rich and decadent.

"You don't sound so excited." He grinned. "I always wondered what those parties were like. Your house always looked so fancy during the holidays. In fact, I saw them starting the decorative work on the exterior yesterday when I passed by."

"So what seems to be the theme this year?" Mary asked.

"Not sure. I saw some silver ribbons, but I didn't look too closely." He studied her a moment, and she squirmed beneath his gaze. "Nonnie and I plan to help decorate the town square this weekend. You should come out."

Her brows rose. "Oh... they still do that, huh?"

"Always." He smiled. "Seems to be a race to see who can have their decorations up the fastest and then everyone gathers to decorate the square. Nonnie and I are in charge of the gazebo this year."

"Sounds like fun." Mary rubbed her hand over her stomach. "I'll have to see what my parents have planned first, but maybe I can swing by." She stood. "I think, now that I am full and filling quite sated by Nonnie's deliciousness, I will head to the house and see my parents... if they're home." She smiled at him. "It was good bumping into you,

Bright. It's been a long time. Welcome back to Ransforth."

"Good to see you too."

She waved at Nonnie.

"Don't you forget to swing by periodically while you're in town, Mary. I love our chats." Nonnie walked around the counter and embraced her once more. Mary returned the hug with fervor.

"I will. I promise. Thank you for the treats." Waving one last time, she darted out the door and to her car to crank up the heat before setting out towards what would be another busy Christmas holiday.

::

"She lives in Landisburg and she only comes home once a year?" Bright turned towards Nonnie in bewilderment as he watched Mary Rutherford back her car out into the street and head towards her parent's home. "That's only a couple of hours away."

"She doesn't have as strong of ties to Ransforth as you do, sweetie." Nonnie retrieved the dirty mugs and plates and walked them to the sink in the back of the shop, Bright following.

"Her parents live here."

"Yes, well... Mary has a unique relationship with her parents."

Bright watched as Nonnie tended to the dishes and dried her hands on a Christmas-themed hand towel. Her apron, a frilly candy cane striped mass of ruffles, was lightly dusted with flour. She untied it from behind her back and draped it on a hook near the door. "I don't understand how someone could barely visit their parents."

"That would be hard for you to understand." Nonnie patted him on the arm as she walked back to the front of the shop, unplugged her Christmas tree lights, and locked the front door. She flipped the handcrafted sign to 'closed' and then began cleaning the table with a damp washcloth. "You grew up in a loving home, nurtured and encouraged by your parents. Mary, while having her physical needs met, didn't have quite the same relationship with her parents as you do yours."

Contemplative, Bright sat in one of the empty chairs. "She used to work here in high school, right?"

"A couple of days a week. She'd wash the dishes, sweep the floors..." Nonnie looked up and smiled as if remembering the good ol' days.

"You've never hired anyone else, and you never hired anyone before her. Why did you hire her?"

Bright asked, studying his grandmother as she continued her nightly routine.

"She needed a place she could be herself. Mary's a sweet girl. Determined and driven, she always strived to live up to her parent's expectations. Sometimes that was hard to do."

"She didn't seem too excited to be heading home."

Sighing, Nonnie looked over at him. "Brighten, please get to the point. You want to know something, then ask, but don't hem and haw over it."

He smirked. "Alright." Pausing, he waited until Nonnie went back to wiping down counters. "She seemed downtrodden, and that just surprised me since it is almost Christmas time. Most people are excited about spending time with family during the holidays. It just perplexes me, that's all."

"Perhaps while she is in town you can introduce her to some fun Christmas activities. She rarely experienced them as a child. The Rutherford's focus during this time is their big holiday celebration, not town parades or events. It might do Mary some good to see what Ransforth has to offer other than a deep-seated dread."

Nonnie reached for her purse. "Now, are you going to give your old granny a ride home, or are you going to just sit there and keep yappin' my ear off?"

Bright grinned as he stood. "Don't get sassy with me, old lady." He draped his arm over Nonnie's shoulders and gave her a firm squeeze before they both dressed for the weather and headed out towards his truck.

Silence hung only briefly as they made their way towards Nonnie's home on the outskirts of town. It was the house he'd loved visiting as a child. His Nonnie and Pappy were two of the best people he'd ever known. And despite losing his Pappy seven years ago, Nonnie's house still ranked as one of his favorite places. That's why, when he'd decided to move back to Ransforth, he'd asked if he could stay with her until he found a place of his own. So far, she'd been quite a delightful roommate. His sister, Grace, continually teased him for living with their grandmother, but in good fun, knowing it was for both their good to have some company.

He'd left California six months prior, the time having flown as soon as he stepped back onto familiar soil. His heart, bitter and angry, directed itself towards Nonnie's house for the tender loving care it knew it needed. Nonnie loved easily and genuinely. Children of all ages loved Nonnie, and her beautiful heart loved them in return. Much like Mary. Mary had been one of Nonnie's children growing up. And even now, as soon as she returned to town, Mary found herself at Nonnie's first as well. He understood that need for Nonnie's warmth and care. And he was thankful he could call her his family. He hadn't realized Mary struggled so much with her upbringing during school. In his mind, the Rutherfords were the dream family. The mansion at the edge of town seemed like a fairytale to pretty much every kid besides Mary. At Halloween, Bright and his siblings made the Rutherford mansion their first stop. They were the type of house that offered full size candy bars that were every child's dream to put in their bucket. But now that he thought about it, he never recalled seeing Mary trick or treating, and the only people he remembered handing out candy were the household staff, not Mr. and Mrs. Rutherford. Odd how looking back with a grownup's perspective sharpened the memories.

"It is a lovely home."

He cast a glance towards the black wrought iron fence that lined the entire Rutherford property, the house lit up with yard lights as dusk turned to dark. He spotted Mary's car in the circle drive, lights still on as if she'd just pulled in. The entry gate was still open and before he could think, he whipped his truck into the drive.

"What on earth, Bright?" Nonnie gripped her door as the sharp turn took her by surprise.

He pulled in behind Mary's car as she exited the house with two men dressed in pressed shirts and slacks. They retrieved her luggage from her trunk. She glanced up in surprise as he hopped out of his truck.

"Bright?" She looked past him and offered a wave to Nonnie. "What are you doing here?"

"Inviting you to breakfast tomorrow." He fisted his hands in his pockets to warm them.

"Oh." She blinked before responding. "That'd be nice."

"Good. I'll pick you up at eight."

She tucked her hair behind her ear. "Actually, can I meet you somewhere? I have to stop by my father's office in the morning."

"Sure. Meet me at Nonnie's at eight."

"I can do that." Finally, a smile spread over her face.

"Excuse me, Ms. Mary," one of the men interrupted. "Are there anymore bags?" He pointed towards the interior of her car and she shook her head.

"No, thank you, Edgar. That will be all." The man nodded and disappeared into the house.

"He seems nice." Bright looked through the front door at the grand entrance to the house. The black and white checked floors, the winding staircases; a different life than he was used to, that was for sure. Mary's parents were nowhere in sight.

"He is. Or at least I think he is. He's new since last year, so I don't really know him."

"Well, I will let you get settled in so you can visit with your parents." Bright nodded towards his truck. "Besides, Nonnie will invite herself in if I don't leave."

Mary chuckled. "She's always welcome. I'll see you tomorrow." Shyly, Mary nodded a farewell and handed her keys to an awaiting attendant before walking into the looming house.

Bright slid behind the wheel of his truck.

"And what was this little detour about?"

"I'm going to make her breakfast at your shop in the morning."

"Oh, is that so?" Nonnie studied his side profile with profound interest. "And what made you decide to do that?"

He shrugged. "Just want to catch up."

Smothering a smile, Nonnie nodded in approval. "I'll be sure to have a hot pot of coffee, then." She reached over and patted his arm as they wound their way through the immaculately landscaped front yard and back towards the road.

:::

The smell of freshly ground coffee summoned Mary from her bedroom at a quarter to six. She followed the scent on floating feet, as if her tired body knew instant replenishment awaited just on the other side of the dining room doors. A set of French, elegantly engraved glass doors opened into the dining room, where a long mahogany table with sparkling white dishes set for three welcomed her. Her father sat in his seat, his electronic tablet opened and propped up next to him. He tapped the screen vigorously as he worked. Her mother breezed into the room carrying an oversized floral arrangement that she sat on the corresponding mahogany buffet table. She looked up to see Mary and smiled. "Morning. Angela told me you made it in last night. How was the drive?"

"Quick and painless." Mary reached for the coffee carafe, but her hand was intercepted by one of the maids who poured it for her before doing the same for her father and mother. She had forgotten how it was to be served, even for the simple task of pouring coffee. "You look great, Mom."

Molly Rutherford fluffed a hand over her platinum blonde updo and beamed. "Thanks, sweetie. I went blonde this summer and I have to say, I am loving it. Rowan, we are at the table, stow the tablet."

Her father tapped a few more times on the screen and then nudged his tablet to the side, though not out of reach. It was then he realized Mary had been sitting beside him at the table. He started at her presence and then smiled. "Morning, Mary. I trust you slept well?"

"Yes, thank you."

"We have a busy day ahead of us," her father began, nodding towards Molly. "Your mother needs help with the preparations for the Christmas party. It would seem she is a bit behind schedule."

"Through no fault of my own," her mother replied. "It seems that our usual caterer forgot to confirm the date of the party when I scheduled it months ago, so I'm without a caterer. Unfortunately, everyone is booked this close to Christmas."

"It's December fourth," Mary began. "Surely there is someone. There's still plenty of time."

"Oh no, if you do not have your caterer booked by August, you're doomed." Molly panicked. "I've called six different caterers, even the two in Landisburg, and all are booked solid through the New Year."

"Have you looked locally?" Mary asked, though she knew the answer. Her mother's answering scoff told her that no, she hadn't looked locally, because why would she.

"This is the biggest party of the year, Mary, for the company and for this town."

"Exactly. That's why I think it would be a great idea to look for a caterer from this town. Support local business."

"There's no way a local shop could handle a party of this magnitude."

"But have you given them a chance?"

"A chance to ruin it? No, I haven't. And I do not intend to. I need you to reach out to any contacts you may have in Landisburg and surrounding areas. I need to have a caterer booked by tomorrow."

"Tomorrow? That's a bit of a steep deadline." Mary took a sip of her coffee.

"Deadlines establish who is in charge," her father stated. "You set the deadline and expectation. If they can't make up their mind by the deadline you give them, then they are not worth your time."

"Geez, Dad, when did you get so hard?" Mary's flippant comment had her dad's head snapping up from his paper. She avoided his gaze. "I'll see what I can do. Anything else?"

"Yes. I ordered the décor months ago and only half of the shipment has arrived."

"Did you call them?" Mary asked.

"No. That's on your list for today." Her mother handed her a clipboard and Mary's heart sank at the sight of the two pages of assignments.

"Your father wants to show you the distribution center this morning. Don't be late, you have a schedule to keep." Her mother narrowed her eyes at Mary until she received the obedient nod she was looking for. She also noticed her mother study her a moment longer than per her usual, and a softness temporarily tinged her gaze before All-Business-Molly fell back into place. "Oh, and I set out a new pantsuit for you."

"I packed clothes, Mom." Mary took a bite of the crispy granola in front of her, not wanting to eat too much so she'd be hungry for breakfast with Bright.

"Yes, I know. But if you are to be representing Rutherford's over the next couple of days, you need to dress in business attire. Have a good day, sweetie." She took the travel mug in well-polished hands from the timid maid who entered the dining hall. Molly bent and kissed Rowan's upturned cheek before exiting.

"Where's she headed this morning?" Mary asked curiously.

"Your mother has her own list to take care of." He reached for his tablet now that his wife was gone, and Mary knew a dismissal when she saw it. She stood.

"I'll dress and head to town. See you at the center at ten, Dad."

"Sure thing." He never glanced up as she exited.

When she opened the door to her bedroom suite, a white pantsuit, perfectly tailored, was hung from a rolling clothing rack and cart that had been wheeled inside. The white pantsuit, black stiletto heels, and a black high-end purse graced the cart. Her mother had thought of everything. Mary quickly dressed, and though it annoyed her how much she liked the look of the outfit, she also felt a small wave of disappointment flutter over her. She was familiar with the Christmas blues. She'd felt them every year as a child, wishing that one day she'd get to experience Christmas like normal families did. Wake up, excited to see what Santa had brought her, eat a big breakfast, and then spend the day playing with her new toys and her parents showering her with attention and joy. But that wasn't the Rutherford way. Typically, the big

Christmas Eve party ended in the early hours of the morning. Her personal gifts, never placed under a tree with the staged decorative gifts, were delivered to her bedroom and placed before the foot of her bed. She opened them by herself before heading down to eat breakfast by herself as her parents slept in and caught up on their sleep from the previous night's festivities. She'd learned to stifle the disappointment over the years. She'd even learned that though she may not enjoy Christmas in her own home, that Christmas festivities elsewhere brought her some seasonal joy. She loved parades. She loved seeing the community come together for fun and laughter and holiday spirit.

Her heels echoed down the stairwell and she slipped into the long peacoat her mother had chosen for her and left with the attendant at the front entry. Dressed for success, Mary headed out into the cold.

« CHAPTER TWO »

"Those sure smell good." Nonnie patted Bright on the back as she walked behind him to grab a tray of freshly decorated reindeer cookies.

"A gooey cinnamon roll is the best way to start the morning."

"And you make the best," Nonnie bragged.

"Now that is a lie, Nonnie." Bright winked at her. "We all know you make the best. Though I hope these at least give Mary a pick me up."

"Do you think she needs one?"

"Seemed like it."

The Christmas jingle sounded as the door to the shop was opened. Nonnie bustled out and Bright listened to make sure it wasn't Mary just yet. He still needed to ice the cinnamon rolls with the rich and delicious cream cheese icing he'd prepared. He plated two of the jumbo rolls and placed them in the warming oven. He'd fetch them when Mary arrived and serve them with fresh, hot coffee. Which, with the freshly falling snow, would be a welcome respite, he was sure. He walked out from the back kitchen and smiled in greeting as Nonnie bagged several pecan tarts for the woman at the register.

"And here's a little sweet for you to have for later." Nonnie placed a snickerdoodle in the bag as well. The woman glanced up at Bright's entry and her smile widened at the sight of him.

"Brighten Smith," she greeted. "Wow, it's been ages."

He recognized her smile immediately and found himself surprised at her presence. "Emily Downs?"

"That's me. But it's Emily Higgins now, though not for long." Her devilish grin told him all he needed to know on that front. "It looks like California treated you well. I'd heard you were back in town but hadn't had the chance to call on you. I wasn't sure where you were staying. I moved back a couple of years ago. It took some adjusting, but it's been good for me and my son."

"You have a son?" Bright asked curiously.

"I do. Max. He's ten and rambunctious, as all little boys should be."

"That's great. I'm happy to see you doing so well." Bright leaned back against the counter and crossed his arms over his chest.

"Do you have children?" Emily asked, her brow quirking just slightly as she fished for more information about him.

"No, I do not. I haven't had the honor yet."

"Ah, well, I'm sure one day you will. Are you seeing anyone?"

Before he could reply, the door opened and Mary stepped inside, her dark hair dusted with a powdered coating of snowflakes. She shimmied away the chill as she untied the coat tied around her waist. His eyes sparked when he saw her dressed in an elegant suit perfectly tailored to her trim figure. Emily eyed her with curiosity until acknowledgement hit her. "My, my, my! Mary Rutherford, is that you?"

Mary glanced up and offered a polite smile. "Good morning."

"Emily," she explained with a hand over her chest. "Emily Downs. From high school."

"Ah." Mary's reply held a sense of hesitancy as she faced off with the one girl who had bullied her in her preteen years. "Good to see you, Emily."

"Love your bag."

"Thanks." Mary looked to Nonnie and beamed. "Morning, Nonnie."

"Good morning, sweetie. Have a seat and I'll bring you a fresh cup of coffee."

"That would be wonderful. Incredible, in fact. It is freezing out there." She sat down in one of the free chairs and opened her purse, retrieving her clipboard and a pen. She cast Bright a look as he held up his finger to signal that he'd be a moment longer.

"I hear this year's Christmas party is to be the best one yet," Emily stated, walking towards Mary's table. "I look forward to it."

"Oh, do you work for R&S?" Bright asked.

Beaming, Emily placed her manicured hand on her chest in pride. "Yes, in acquisitions, directly under Mr. Rutherford."

"I'm sure I will see you later then," Mary replied. "I'm swinging by his office at ten."

"Wonderful." Emily's smile was forced as she reached inside her purse to retrieve her car keys. "I'll make sure Mr. Rutherford knows."

"He does. He's the one that scheduled it." Mary looked up and beamed at the giant cinnamon roll headed her direction. Bright slid into the seat across from her with his own roll and looked up at Emily.

"Well, you two enjoy your morning. It was great to see you, Bright." She rested a hand on his shoulder a moment before power strutting outside.

"Nice to know my father's number two is Emily Downs." Mary grimaced and Bright laughed.

"I see her being quite the dedicated employee," Bright added. "She always loved life at the top of the pecking order."

"Don't I know it."

"So what's this?" Bright tapped her clipboard and she mustered an enthusiastic response. "This is my to-do list."

He cringed on her behalf. "May I?" He hesitated a moment before she nodded and then grabbed the clipboard. "Wow, looks like you have your work cut out for you."

"I do. Top of my list is finding a caterer for the big party. Apparently, that was messed up somehow and my mom is freaking out over it."

"A caterer for Christmas Eve?"

"Yep. Shouldn't be too difficult right?" Nervous laughter drifted from her lips as she ran her hands through her hair. "I don't know how I'm going to find someone. And on top of that, half of my mom's decorations haven't arrived, so that will be phone call number two this morning."

"And this is all that's needed?" He pointed to a separate list attached to the back of the first.

"Yes."

"One hundred wrapped gift boxes?"

"For under the trees throughout the house."

"What's inside them?" Bright asked.

"Nothing."

"They're *empty*?"

She laughed. "Yep. They're just meant to look pretty around the tree."

"So where do your family gifts go?"

She shrugged. "A closet, I guess, until Christmas morning."

"So you have to find a hundred empty boxes, wrap them, and stage them?"

"Yes."

He rubbed a hand over his jaw. "What if... what if the boxes weren't empty?"

"What do you mean?"

"What if you did a toy drive or something? And guests brought a wrapped gift to put under the tree."

Mary leaned back in her chair with a small smile. "That's a brilliant idea. However, I'm not sure my mother would go for it. She would want everything to be wrapped in corresponding colors to the tree."

"That picky, is she?"

"You have no idea." Mary took a bite of her cinnamon roll and sighed. "This is fantastic, thank you."

"Don't mention it. Figured it would be a pick me up for this cold morning."

"Especially since I have a lot to d—" She paused and then her face lit up. "Hold the phone!" She waved her hands excitedly for him to hand her the clipboard. "What *if* we had a gift wrapping station? People could bring their toy donations and we could have a table to the side where they could wrap it themselves or I could have a few staff members there to do it for them. Then, I could order the correct paper and colors to match my mother's theme, but we could also still do something great with the gifts?"

Bright grinned. "And that, Mary Rutherford, is an awesome idea." He toasted his coffee mug towards her.

She scribbled her notes down. "I could order the wrappings today and that's one less thing on my list!" She did a small jig in her seat and he laughed. "Thank you for your help!"

"I didn't do anything," Bright chuckled.

"You did! The toy drive idea is brilliant. If we're going to have half the town at the party, then we might as well do something for the community. There are plenty of kids who would love to have a new toy for Christmas. I'll talk to the school and see who they recommend we reach out to."

"You're on a roll."

Her face dimmed a bit. "I'm sorry." She nudged her clipboard aside. "The only roll I should be focusing on is this cinnamon one. I'm as bad as my dad, bringing work to the table."

"Hey, I'm glad we were able to get you started."

"It's a brilliant idea, the toys. I don't know why my parents hadn't thought of it before."

"Well, if you need any other great ideas, you know who to come to."

She grinned. "That I do. So tell me about California. How'd you like it there?"

Bright tilted his head to the side trying to think of at least one positive answer. "It has fantastic weather."

Laughing, she took a sip of her coffee. "Is that all?"

"Pretty much." He smirked at her exaggerated eye roll.

"Well, where did you live? Let's start with that."

"San Diego."

"I hear they have beautiful beaches."

"There is that. Living near the ocean was fun. I enjoyed morning runs along the water."

"Sounds dreamy compared to my humid jogs through the park in Landisburg."

"Hey, that sounds nice compared to San Diego. I hear Landisburg has nice trees," Bright added.

"Are you seriously saying Landisburg city park trees are better than California beaches?" Mary laughed. "Have you hit your head recently?" She reached across the table as if checking him for fever.

Laughing, he swatted her hand away. "Maybe I'm a little bitter about San Diego."

"Must be." She grinned despite his statement and he smiled, thankful she didn't push for more information on the subject. Instead, she clapped her hands and began gathering her things.

"Well, I better head out. I've got to meet my dad at ten at his office. I can't wait to share our idea with him."

"Your idea," Bright reminded her.

"I can't take full credit." She pointed at him. "And if it turns into a massive undertaking, I'm going to force you to help me with it."

"I'll freely sign myself up. Let me know if there is anything I can do to help, Mary, honestly."

Shouldering her purse, she nodded. "Don't worry, I will." She gave him a conspiratorial wink as she waved towards Nonnie and ducked her way outside into the cold.

::

"We've expanded our acquisitions department to the second and third floors now."

Her father droned on about the recent updates at R&S Distribution and Mary, though offering the accolades she knew her father wanted to hear, was genuinely impressed with the increase in numbers from the previous year. Her father had almost doubled their client base in the last nine months alone, and the expansions for acquisitions and distribution just made logical sense.

"Emily has done a great job heading the acquisitions department. Our numbers are through the roof thanks to her." He nodded his approval to Emily as she walked alongside them through the distribution floor.

"I am impressed with all you've done, Dad. Glad to see you have had such a fantastic year."

Rowan nodded his dismissal towards Emily, and she wandered off as he motioned to the door of his office and for Mary to enter inside. "Have you been working on your list?"

"Yes. In fact, I have a great idea for the party, but I'm not sure Mom will like it."

His brow rose as he steepled his fingers and leaned back in his office chair. "Oh?"

"Yeah... So I was thinking it would be great to do a toy drive this year. Mom always has gift boxes wrapped and planted under all the trees, but what if we actually *filled* the boxes this year? People would bring a toy when they come, there'd be a wrapping station set up, and then the gift could be placed under one of the trees."

Rowan listened as she began listing various organizations in Ransforth and surrounding towns that would benefit from the gift donations. She'd covered all the bases: Child Protective Services, children's homes, shelters. When she'd finished rattling off her list, she looked up to find him smiling at her.

"And the catering situation?"

"I'm still on that one." She frowned. "That might be tough if Mom doesn't want to use anyone local."

"Your mother assigned the task to you. It no longer matters what she'd prefer. If she wants to choose the caterer, then she should have put that on her list."

"But Dad, you know how picky she is."

"Mary, the task is yours. All I ask is that it be delicious. Last year's caterer was a disaster. Though your mother liked the food, the rest of the people did not. Not many people around here have a palate for caviar."

Mary feigned a grossed-out expression and he chuckled. "Exactly. Know your audience."

"I've got an idea, actually. We do live in the south, and the south *knows* food. One of the best things about holidays is the food. That's the time you get to have special dishes, rich and decadent food you wouldn't normally eat year round. I thought about finding someone who's able to make those traditional delicious dishes and perhaps set up a buffet."

"A buffet?"

She could tell he hated the idea. "In good taste," she amended. "It won't be casserole dishes lined up like a potluck, I promise."

He chuckled. "Very well, I look forward to seeing what you come up with. But for heaven's sake, don't tell your mother you are planning a buffet. She'd have a stroke."

"Is there anything else you want me to take care of for you, besides what's on my list?"

"No, Mary, I think that will be all."

"Well, thanks for the tour of the center. I like the changes you've implemented. They're smart and tangible and seem to already be positively impacting the business."

"Yes. It's been a good year. A busy one, but good." He sighed as his desk phone rang. It was then she studied him as he held up his finger for silence to answer. As he talked into the receiver, Mary noticed the fine lines around his eyes that she hadn't remembered being there the year before. The small bags beneath his eyes spoke of tiredness or restlessness, she wasn't sure which. *How had she not noticed that this morning?*

He hung up and stood, buttoning his suit jacket. "Well, I have a schedule to keep. You have a list to take care of. Let's say we reconvene at dinner this evening?"

Mary nodded. "Sure." She stuffed her clipboard in the black purse her mother had assigned her that morning and stood. "By this evening I will have the caterer booked."

"I like your enthusiasm, Mary, and your determination." He smiled as she studied him a moment longer.

"And Dad?"

He tilted his head. "Yes?"

She paused a moment, not sure what to say, just that she hated seeing him so tired and worn. "Drink some water today, huh? No more coffee." She pointed at the empty mugs lining the left side of his desk.

He nodded as he chuckled. "Sure thing, sweetie."

She closed his office door and headed towards her car. If she was to have the caterer booked by this evening, she had some begging to do. And beg she would.

The drive from the distribution center into town was short and she whipped her car into a parking spot outside of Nonnie's as several people exited with warm drinks and treats, and most importantly, smiles. She hurried from her car to the door and then darted back, reaching inside for the black bag on her passenger seat before hurrying back towards Nonnie's. As she turned from her car, she slammed into Bright's chest.

"Whoa there, Steve McQueen, what's the rush?"

"Oh, Bright," Mary swiped her hair out of her eyes. "I'm glad you're here. Come with me." Her eyes danced as she grabbed his hand and dragged him inside his grandmother's shop. When the door closed behind them, Mary waited patiently for Nonnie to finish up with a customer before she pounced... more like bounced, her nerves and excitement had her so jittery.

Nonnie glanced up and smiled. "I take it your visit with your father went well?" she asked.

"Yes." Mary beamed.

"And he liked the toy drive idea?" Nonnie asked.

"Yes." Mary waved away their current topic. "There's something else, Nonnie."

Nonnie watched as Mary retrieved her clipboard out of her purse.

"I can tell I'm going to need another cup of coffee for this chat, aren't I?"

Smiling, Mary nodded. "Bright too."

"Oh boy." Bright rubbed a hand over the back of his neck before pointing to one of the small tables. He pulled an extra chair towards the table as Nonnie walked over three mugs of hot brew.

"Now, tell me what's got you in a tizzy," Nonnie ordered.

"I have an enormous favor to ask you. Well, both of you, I guess, because we're going to need your help, Bright."

"Alright, what is it?" Nonnie asked, Mary's excitement already spreading to her.

"I want you to cater the R&S Distribution Christmas party."

Nonnie and Bright both leaned back in their chairs, silent, and watchful as Mary began sharing her ideas about dishes and set up.

"Now, I will have everything set up, you guys would just need to worry about the food. But if there are certain heating pans, bowls, dishes, etc. I can handle those. Oh, and we are looking at a guest list of around 400 people, so we would need t—"

Bright held up a hand. "Whoa, Mary, slow down a minute."

She faltered at his interruption and looked up to see that neither of them looked to be excited about the idea. "Is something wrong?"

"Honey," Nonnie reached forward and gripped her hand. "the party is on Christmas Eve."

"Yes." Mary nodded, not seeing the problem.

"We have family activities on Christmas Eve," Nonnie explained. "We won't be able to cater for you. I'm sorry."

Mary's face fell. "But Nonnie, your food is the best. Your cookies, cakes, pies, and anything you've ever made is delicious."

"And I thank you for that sweet compliment, but I wish to spend the holiday with my family, not rushin' around cooking for 400 people."

Mary ran a hand through her hair and fluffed it, a nervous habit, as she wondered what she was going to do now. She felt her hands start to shake as anxiety over trying to find another catering option loomed over her. "I understand." She forced a smile.

Bright sat quietly studying her and she felt embarrassed at just assuming they'd want to take on such a project.

"I'll do it," Bright said.

Nonnie and Mary turned to him in surprise.

He raised his shoulders. "What? I know all of Nonnie's recipes. I could do it."

"For 400 people?" Mary asked. "And you're a part of Nonnie's family, Bright, don't you want to be with family on Christmas Eve?"

"I will be. I may just have to cut my visit short."

"Oh, I couldn't ask you to do that." Mary shook her head and he held up his hands.

"Mary, you need a caterer. I can do it. I've helped Nonnie in the past. Besides, I will have all of Christmas day to spend with family." He looked to Nonnie and she nodded her consent. "Besides, most of the treats can be frozen up until the day of the party. Cookies, cakes, and pies can be frozen, so if we start soon, we will have plenty ready to go. The hot dishes, depending on what you have planned, can be prepared a couple of days ahead and then baked or fried the day of the party."

"Are you sure?"

"I am. That is, *if* you want to hire me. I know I'm not your typical caterer, and we would have to do some major teamwork, because as far as plates, cups, napkins—"

"I'll take care of those." Mary brightened. "All I need you to worry about is the food. I'll even handle the drinks." She reached over and squeezed his hand on a light squeal. "We've got this, Bright."

"I'm looking forward to it."

"And thank you." She stood, her nerves now shifted into eager anticipation of starting her drafts of the menu she'd like prepared. "You Smiths are the best." She gave Nonnie a peck on the cheek and then did the same to Bright. "I will touch base with you first thing in the morning, Bright. I'll figure out a menu tonight and we can go over it tomorrow. Are you free?"

"I'll be here." He smiled as she all but jumped in place. "Okay, see you then." She hurried out, the afternoon sun slightly halting the steady drifts of snow that had blanketed the town overnight. A white Christmas seemed more charming somehow. She slid behind the wheel of her car and looked over her checklist. Next up: facing her mother.

« CHAPTER THREE »

"Brighten Smith, have you hit your head?" Nonnie asked as soon as Mary stepped out onto the sidewalk. "You don't know a thing about catering, much less the biggest party of the year for this town."

"That's why you're going to help me." He winked at her.

"And when will I do that? I have a shop to run."

"Nonnie," Bright reached for her hands. "I can do it."

"I have no doubts you can, I just don't think you realize the gravity of the situation you're in. That girl has put her hopes in you. If you fail her, she will never forget it."

"So I won't fail her."

"I know you won't intentionally, but 400 people is an enormous workload."

"Then I guess I better get started." He reached for a notepad. "What do you recommend for cookies?"

Nonnie sat silent a moment and then threw up her hands. "Very well. I will help you when I can, but make this your mantra, young man."

He leaned in to listen closely.

"Keep it simple."

"That's it?"

"That's it." Nonnie gave an affirming nod of her head. "Choose four cookies and those are the only ones you're going to make. That gives options without stressing you out by making dozens of different cookies. Same for the pies and cakes. Keep it simple. Four choices of each."

"I like that idea. Will also be easier to keep track."

"Yes. Now, I know Mary is going to think up some foods, but you also don't be afraid to say no if something is out of your wheelhouse. Those parties are fancy, so I'm sure the food will need to be as well. Are you prepared for that?"

"Can I dig into your recipe box?" Bright asked.

"I don't have recipes for the likes of R&S Distribution."

"I could modify some, surely." He was starting to feel the beginning stages of panic. *He could do this. Couldn't he? What had made him volunteer? What was he thinking? He knew why.* And if Nonnie wanted him to keep things simple, then that's what his reason was. The reason he volunteered was because of Mary. Simple. He wanted to be near her, get to know her, and help her. And he had to admit, that her crestfallen face when Nonnie told her no had twisted his gut. *He couldn't sit by when she needed help, right?*

"You're a good man, Bright." Nonnie patted his hand. "Just don't be a stupid one. Be smart, be honest, and keep it simple," she reminded him.

"I will. That's great advice, Nonnie."

"And be kind to Mary."

"Of course. Why wouldn't I be?"

"I just know the holidays are hard for her and with her having to plan part of her parent's party, she is likely to be under some extra stress. I want her to be able to enjoy her holiday."

"All the more reason why I should help her out. It takes part of that stress away." Bright grinned. "Besides, it will be fun to reconnect with Mary."

Nonnie watched as he began scribbling down his thoughts on the notepad and smothered her smile. "I think that would be wonderful. Mary is a sweet girl."

"She seems like it. She was quiet in high school. I vaguely remember working on a project together one semester in biology, but for the most part we only saw each other in passing. She was never at any of the parties or school events. I'm not even sure she went to prom."

"She didn't," Nonnie stated. "She was here with me."

"Why?" Bright looked confused. "I mean, no offense Nonnie, you're great, but prom is what high schoolers look forward to all year."

"Her parents did not wish for her to go. She had an image to upkeep."

"Image?"

"Business-oriented," Nonnie explained.

"She was seventeen!" Bright shook his head in disbelief. "What seventeen-year-old thinks about business? And why would she need to?"

"She's a Rutherford, and with that comes responsibilities."

"She's not Spiderman for crying out loud!" Bright, enraged that Mary had missed out on such things as prom for the sake of the family business, felt heat rise to his face. "That is the most ridiculous thing I've ever heard. And for her to miss out on that and then not even be a part of the company is even more absurd."

"That's just the way it was, and Mary accepted it."

"I wouldn't have." Defiantly, Bright stood and walked to the coffee pot to top off his mug.

"You say that because you didn't have to make that choice and you were not raised how Mary was raised. But hopefully you can understand why she is so eager to please her parents with this party."

"I certainly understand, though if I were her, I'd just turn the shoulder and run in the opposite direction."

"From your parents?" Nonnie asked.

Bright shook his head. "You're right, I wouldn't, but her parents need a good shaking."

Nonnie chuckled. "I thought that about your parents a time or two when you were younger."

"Why? What did I or they ever do?"

"For starters they bought you that brand-new Mustang when you turned sixteen and you drove it like a race car driver." She shook her head in dismay and then smiled up at him. "We all have moments in our lives that, upon reflection, take on a whole new view."

"I was responsible with that car, even at sixteen," Bright defended, though without conviction.

"Oh really?" Nonnie laughed. "Is that how it came to be wrapped around a telephone pole? I believe you were in a leg cast for eleven weeks, am I right?"

He flushed. "Okay, so I wasn't that smart with it. And maybe an older vehicle would have been a better choice for me so that my ego would have stayed in check."

Nonnie laughed. "Enough life lessons for today. I believe you have some cookies to make."

::

Four days in Ransforth and Mary had booked a caterer, and she had her mother's missing decorations arriving just as she stood at the base of the stairs in the entryway sizing up one of the themed Christmas trees. The staff had worked tirelessly the last few days to transform the Rutherford home into a Christmas wonderland of silvers, whites, blues, and deep shades of purple.

Not exactly the traditional Christmas color scheme, but the frosted effect on the place felt as if you'd stepped into a snow-covered crystal palace. She'd made bulk orders of wrapping paper and ribbons for the gifts that the guests would bring, and the order was expected to arrive later in the afternoon. Her list was coming together. She glanced at her watch: an hour before she planned to meet with Bright to go over menu options, which was just enough time to make sure the grand tree was underway in the parlor. She walked through the open French doors into the parlor and her mother stood at the base of the tree as several of the stronger staff members shifted it into place. The tree, a fifteen-foot fir, was the spectacle of the house during Christmas season.

Molly glanced over at her entrance. "What do you think? From there? Where you're standing by the door." She motioned for Mary to take a couple of steps back for a moment. "Is that a decent angle? I thought about setting it up where I did last year, but it was so lost in the corner there. I wanted it to make a statement."

"The middle of the room certainly makes a statement," Mary answered. "I think it's a good spot. It will look lovely once it is decorated."

Molly nodded and waved her hand for the staff to continue setting it up where it stood. Mary noticed several relieved glances as they continued working. "How is everything else coming along?"

"Good. I meet with the caterer in an hour."

"Oh? And who did you find?"

"Brighten Smith." Mary watched as her mother's face instantly paled.

"What?"

"Yes. Nonnie's grandson. He's agreed to do it."

"W-w-what does he know about catering? Isn't he some sort of computer whiz?"

"I don't know about that, but I do know he can cook, and that's what I've hired him to do. I've already spoken to Dad about it."

"Have you?" She looked perplexed that Rowan would even consider such a choice. "Well, I guess if your father said it was okay, then I'm willing to give him a try."

"That's the spirit." Mary lightly punched her mom's arm, her mother eyeing her with even more concern that Mary had to laugh. "Relax, Mom, I know how much this party means to you. I promise I won't screw it up."

"Good. On that note, when the wrappings get here go ahead and have the staff begin wrapping boxes. Did you order boxes? I haven't seen them."

"Oh, that's something else that will be different this year."

Molly Rutherford eased into a chair. "Good Lord, Mary, are you going to kill your mother?"

Mary laughed. "Easy, Mom. I have a plan. On the invitations everyone will be asked to bring a toy to wrap, and then all the gifts will be donated to various shelters and organizations for kids to have for the holidays."

"A charity event, then?"

"Yes. Also approved by Dad," Mary added quickly.

Her mother's shoulders relaxed, and she reached for Mary's hand. "I think that's a wonderful idea. Just as long as they all match under the tree."

"That is why we will have a wrapping center set up over here." Mary walked her mother to a corner separate from the main party mingling areas. "They can wrap their own gift, or we will have staff here to do it for them. Then the gifts will be placed under the trees. The parlor tree will be the main focus. We'll surround the base of it first since it is such a focal point."

Her mother nodded as she envisioned Mary's plan. "I think that will work. But what if people forget to bring a toy, or worse, what if they do but we don't have enough. Oh, Mary..." Her mother fretted and walked out of the room and hurried back inside with her purse. She fished around inside and withdrew a black credit card. "I want you to go buy some toys and we'll have some already under the tree when people arrive. That way they can see we also donated to the cause."

Mary accepted the card. "How much do you want to spend?"

Molly waved her hand. "How about fifty toys. Twenty-five for boys and twenty-five for girls. The staff can wrap them."

"Alright." Mary added the task of shopping for toys to her list.

"I have full confidence in you, Mary. I think this year's party will be fabulous. As long as Brighten makes wonderful food."

"He will. I promise."

::

"Okay, so I'm a little out of practice." Bright slid the pan of burnt gingerbread men to the counter and Nonnie fanned a dish towel in the air. "What did I do wrong?"

"I would think the answer would be quite obvious." Nonnie giggled. "You cooked them too long."

Bright narrowed his gaze at her as she laughed. "Sweetie, I told you 8-10 minutes in the oven."

"Well, I had to go grab something out of the truck, and then the coffee needed to be brewed."

"Let me worry about the front of the shop. You just work on this." Nonnie pointed to the burnt cookies. "Mary will be here in 45 minutes. If you're wanting to impress her with samples, you will need to stay focused."

"I hear ya." Bright sighed as he grabbed a fresh baking sheet and began placing round two of cookies to bake onto the pan. He'd successfully made the other three kinds of cookies he hoped to win her approval with, but the gingerbread men were giving him a hard time. He could change his plan for those and make a different cookie instead, but gingerbread men felt like Christmas. They smelled like Christmas. And he was just stubborn enough that he didn't want to give up on them.

He heard the Christmas carol float through the air signaling the front door of the shop opening. He heard Nonnie's greeting and he quickly shoved the burnt cookies into the trash before Mary walked into the kitchen. She was early and he was not going to let her see his failed attempts.

She smiled. "Smells... somewhat good in here."

He flushed. "I had a mishap earlier."

"Ah." She chuckled. "I know I'm early but thought I would swing by any way. My mom has given me another task, so if I can meet with you a little earlier than planned, I can get started on the next thing."

"No problem. Though you will need to sit back here for the next 8-10 minutes because I'm determined to get these cookies just right."

"I can do that." She eased onto a stool and set her purse by her feet. "So, I drafted a sample menu."

"Me too. Let me grab my notebook." He walked towards the back entrance and grabbed a blue spiral notebook underneath his keys. "Now, I do have a few questions."

"Okay, ask away."

"Will there be servers? Or does everything already need to be sliced and available for a quick pick up?"

"There will be servers behind the tables to assist with anything that we need."

"Perfect, because my thought was to have a few spiral hams as focal dishes across the table."

"I have ham on my list as well, and I like the idea. The servers can slice off pieces for the guests."

"Cheese trays, obviously," he added.

"Yes."

"Deviled eggs."

"Oh thank heavens, yes."

He laughed.

"Please tell me you put mac and cheese on your menu."

He looked up. "I didn't. I thought that might be too informal."

"Oh, it's going on there. And it may be an informal food, but we can make it look beautiful in the silver serving dishes. But to me, it's one of the dishes I look forward to every holiday meal."

"I can add it on there."

"Asparagus?"

"Yep. On there."

"Glazed carrots?"

"Great minds think alike," he added.

"Fresh baked rolls?"

"Of course."

"I think we are on the same page. Whatever else you have planned, just shoot it to me in an email." She reached for his notebook and wrote down her email address. "I want people to taste a bit of nostalgia with what we serve. And, if I'm being honest, I want to have the Christmas dinner I've always dreamed of, even if it is at a party."

He knew then that he would move mountains to make every dish superb for her.

"So, how are those cookies?"

He jolted and hurried towards the oven. Perfect. He slid the tray out and she nodded in approval. "Not bad, Mr. Smith."

"I also thought pecan tartlets might be good. Instead of making large pies, I thought individual mini pies of various kinds would be easier to serve and might make for a fun display."

"I like that idea."

"He slid a spatula under one of the gingerbread men and placed it on a tray with other various desserts. "Your samples, Ms. Rutherford."

"Oh my." Her eyes lit up. "I don't even know where to begin."

"I would suggest the delicious and very warm gingerbread man."

Laughing, she lifted the cookie and took a bite. Closing her eyes, she savored, and he waited anxiously before she nodded. "Yes. Definitely put these on the list."

He smiled and pointed at a small custard pie and handed her a fork. She cut through the flaky crust and took a bite. Her eyes rolled a moment. "Is that buttermilk?"

"Yep. A classic, Southern staple."

"Oh my, that's delicious. I could eat a thousand of those."

"Good."

"Bright, this is all so incredible. Did Nonnie help you? Or is this all you?"

"All me." He slipped his hands into his pockets as she took a bite of the pecan tartlet next and drummed her feet on the floor in excitement.

"I had no idea you could bake like this."

"When you grow up with Nonnie as your grandmother, you better believe she taught us her ways."

"And how are you not married yet?" Mary joked as she held a hand to her mouth to prevent a crumb from falling into her lap.

Bright snapped his fingers. "I forgot." He rushed to the refrigerator and grabbed a gallon of milk and poured her a tall glass.

She held up the glass and her eyes sparkled. "Bright, you're a genius."

"Well, thank you."

"No, seriously." She held the glass of milk up. "Why don't we serve cold milk next to the dessert table? Yes, there will be champagne everywhere, wine... but a nice glass of cold milk with your cookies, who doesn't love that?"

"Probably your mother," Bright added, and Mary laughed.

"We can pour it into champagne flutes, that way it will be festive and to her fancy tastes, but I think it would be different and fun." She took a long gulp and nodded. "Yep, we're doing it."

He grinned. "So what else does your mom have you doing today?"

"Buying gifts. She doesn't want the trees to be completely bare when guests arrive, so I'm going toy shopping. Want to go?"

"Right now?"

"Yes. I plan to go to Mr. Destin's shop."

"That big one off the interstate?"

"That's the one."

"Give me a few minutes to finish up this batch of cookies and then I'm all yours."

She stood, grabbing the tray of sugary sweets and her milk. "I'll wait out here, stuffing my face with all of this. Take your time." She walked out to the front and he heard her call Nonnie over to the table to share.

When he pulled the last batch of cookies out of the oven, he wiped down counters, stored the extra cookies, and walked out to find both women poring over Mary's menu plans. Though Nonnie was adamant she wasn't going to help, she couldn't help herself.

Mary looked up. "Ready?"

He nodded. "That is, if you don't need me, Nonnie."

"Nope. You two have fun." She winked at him and he felt his cheeks redden a bit at her insinuation.

"Great." Mary stood, grabbing the tray and walked it back behind the counter into the kitchen to dispose of the leftovers.

"Don't get any ideas, Nonnie," Bright whispered.

Innocently raising her shoulders to her ears, Nonnie denied any sort of notions. "I just think it's wonderful the two of you are enjoying each other's company."

"Right, well, that's all it is." He slid into his coat as Mary walked back into the room. She held up her purse. "I almost forgot this back there. Ready?"

"When you are."

She gave Nonnie a quick hug before heading to her car. "I'll drive since I have more storage space for the toys."

"How many do you plan on buying?"

She reached into her purse and grabbed her mother's credit card holding it up for him to see. She grinned mischievously.

"The world is your oyster, Mary Rutherford." Laughing, she turned the key and pulled out onto the road.

« CHAPTER FOUR »

The automatic doors slid open at their arrival, and immediately the sounds and smells of childhood memories flooded over her. How many times had she walked into this exact toy store as a kid to come and play with all the toys? It was always a special treat to stop by to touch and explore all the different toys that were out on the market. In reality, Mary could have purchased or asked for any toy she wanted, but she never had. Instead, her nanny, whomever possessed the role at the time, would sit in one of the brightly colored chairs in the reading nook while Mary wandered the store and explored on her own. She had a couple of nannies over the years that would pretend play with her amongst the aisles, but for the most part, they kept to themselves. Hours upon hours of being lost in her own imagination, aisle upon aisle of new stories and adventures to explore. She glanced up as Mr. Destin, the store owner walked towards them. His steps were slower, his face sporting more wrinkles, but his familiar sweater vest, khaki pants, and warm smile were the same. His eyes lit up at the sight of Mary. He reached for her hands and squeezed. "Mary Rutherford." She leaned forward and kissed his cheek.

"Hi, Mr. Destin. It's been a long time."

"It sure has." He beamed and then looked up at Bright. Rubbing his chin, he studied Bright a moment. "You are Nonnie Smith's grandson, are you not?"

"Yes sir." Bright extended his hand and Mr. Destin shook it.

"Ah, Brighten, I believe. Star Wars Millennium Falcon... oh, what year was that.... 1990?"

Bright laughed. "1992. Great memory."

Mr. Destin snapped his fingers. "That's right. A special memory for certain. One always remembers when a child's dream comes true. I believe that was a memorable birthday for you."

"It was. It definitely was," Bright agreed.

Mr. Destin looked to Mary. "What can I do you for, Mary?"

"Well, I'm here to buy some presents." Her eyes wandered to the angel tree set up at the front of the store, small paper angels with Christmas gift wishes and hopes listed on the backs. "What happens if you run out of angels?"

Mr. Destin followed her gaze. "Depending on how many days are left before Christmas I could request more, but to be honest, usually I have several left on the tree and I end up fulfilling them. People just don't seem as eager to grant a wish these days."

Mary looked up at Bright and he grinned.

"We'll fulfill them all," she stated. "Along with fifty more."

Mr. Destin's eyes bulged behind his glasses before he burst into joyful laughter. "If you're certain."

"I definitely am." Mary handed Bright a list. "You handle the boy gifts, I'll handle the girls. Is your wife here, Mr. Destin?"

"Always. Barbara is in the back."

"Think she could help you gather the angel gifts?"

"She'd be delighted." He squeezed Mary's hand once more before walking to the tree and removing the small paper angels on display.

Mary grabbed a shopping cart and nudged it towards Bright. "Try and find the coolest gifts you can find. I don't care how much they cost. Whatever you think will make a kid feel special and excited. Just make sure it's not too big and will fit under the tree. No bicycles unless it's an angel gift." She laughed. "My mother would have a fit if a bicycle were not wrapped and under the tree. It would throw off her 'look.'"

"Got it."

"Oh, and Bright?"

"Yes?"

"Try to look at more than just Star Wars stuff, okay?"

His eyes sparkled as he laughed. "I'll try my best."

She watched as he wheeled his cart towards the action figure aisle. She headed straight for the baby dolls. As a girl, she loved baby dolls. She was guilty of having that little girl dream of a doll that she could feed, and it would wet little diapers. But her mother wouldn't allow her to own one. Any toy that made a mess was not a toy, but a chore. So, Mary grabbed two for the cart. Barbara

Destin turned onto the aisle with her own cart and lovingly stretched out her arms as she squealed. She rocked Mary side to side as she squeezed the breath out of her. "Mary, Mary, Mary. I'm so thankful and happy to see you!" She pulled back and lightly fluffed the ends of Mary's hair. "More beautiful every time I see you." Knowing she hadn't seen Mrs. Destin since her teens, Mary was grateful for braces and acne cleanser. "Thank you for granting our angels a wonderful Christmas." Mrs. Destin held up her handful of paper angels.

"You're welcome. Though it's on behalf of R&S Distribution."

"Either way, it's a sweet gesture and these children will feel so special."

"I hope so." The women both turned at the sound of Bright's voice. He was nudging his cart with one hand while he held a toy in the other and read the back of a box out loud. "What do you think?" He held up the action figure and showed her.

"Sounds good to me. I've never heard of that particular hero."

"Seriously?" Bright looked stunned.

"Why? Is it popular?"

"Mary, there's a movie in the theatres about him right now."

"Oh." Sheepishly, she felt her cheeks warm. "I don't go to the movies that often."

"Well, we're going tonight then," Bright stated. "What'd you find?" He peeked into her cart. "Baby dolls, good choice. My nieces love dolls."

Mary warmed at his affirmation of her choice and was thankful the idea of a baby doll for Christmas wasn't outdated.

"I'll let you two get on with your lists." Mrs. Destin winked at them as she turned her cart down the neighboring aisle.

"I'm having a hard time deciding upon gifts," Mary admitted. "I want them all." She laughed. "It's like kid Mary has taken over and all I want to do is fulfill my own selfish wish list."

"Do it. Whatever you wanted as a kid, get it." Bright raised his shoulders and dropped them as he looked at the pink boxes of the various dolls. "If you had that wish as a little girl, I imagine there's another little girl out there with the same one."

His cart held more toys than hers and he handed her his list. "I'm done."

She looked over the toys in his cart. "Doesn't seem like that many."

"You said twenty-five, right?"

"Yeah, but looking at it now, it doesn't seem like that many."

"Don't forget, you're fulfilling the angel tree too. That will add more to the carts."

"Yeah, but those will stay here with Mr. Destin. Let's go ahead and add another twenty-five to each basket."

Bright's brows rose. "You sure? Remember, you're going to have other guests bringing gifts as well."

"I know, but not everyone will bring one. I want to make sure we have enough."

Bright's gaze softened as he rested his hand on her shoulder. "You're a good person, Mary Rutherford."

She flushed and shook away his compliment. "I'm just doing what anyone would do if given the opportunity."

"Are you?" he asked doubtfully. "Pretty sure your family's company has never bought out an angel tree or bought gifts for every shelter and nonprofit in the tri county area before. Are you telling me they are just now able to do that?"

"Well, yeah, I guess they could have, but—"

"But that was before you." He smirked at her and she rolled her eyes as she fluffed her hair, a nervous habit when she felt uncomfortable.

"You're a good person, Mary. I'm rather sorry I didn't get to know you better in high school."

She snickered. "High school was a long time ago. It's probably best you didn't know high school me. I wasn't that great."

"I don't know. The way Nonnie speaks of you, I'd beg to differ."

"Nonnie has a way of only seeing the good in people."

"It's her gift," Bright added, and Mary nodded.

"That it is. She's special to me. If it wasn't for her in high school, I may have turned out quite differently," Mary admitted. "She was a friend when I needed one most."

Their conversation was interrupted by Mr. Destin as he gleefully wheeled his cart towards them. "Mary, I have to say, I've had more fun picking out these toys. I love finding the perfect toy to bring a child joy."

"And you're so good at it," she complimented on a laugh as he rummaged through Bright's cart with a look of approval.

"Apparently I didn't gather enough," Bright reported. "I will wheel around once more for another blitz." He gave a slight elbow nudge at Mary when he walked by and she smiled.

Mr. Destin tilted his head as he studied her. "How are you, Mary?"

She exhaled a long breath. "Good for the most part. Just trying to prep for the big holiday party. You and Mrs. Destin should come this year," she invited and felt her shoulders sag as he shook his head. "Why not?" she asked.

"The party is for R&S employees, Mary." He chuckled. "I'm far from that."

"Not everyone there will be R&S people. I will be there," she pointed out before smiling hopefully.

"You're sweet to ask us, but we will have a house full of grandchildren on Christmas Eve. And that's when I have my moment." He paused for dramatic affect. "Grandpa's famous hot cocoa is always the treat before bed on Christmas Eve. It fills little tummies with warm Christmas wishes and that's how Santa knows what gifts to bring." He winked at her as she tenderly smiled.

"That sounds magical."

"To the grandkids, it is. And for me, I will admit. There's nothing better than sharing Christmas with family." Realizing what he said and feeling guilty that he confessed that to Mary Rutherford, the lonely little girl of Christmases past, he cleared his throat and pretended to gaze over the angel papers in his hands.

"This place was magical to me as a kid." She reached out and placed her hand on his. "I would walk in those doors and escape for hours. I played. I imagined. I wished. It was always the perfect gift, even for just a few hours. I thank you for that."

"Oh, now, Mary. You know we loved having you come in."

She grinned. "Yes, you did, and I'm thankful for that too."

His eyes glistened a moment before he gathered himself. "Look at me, an old man blubbering. We've got gifts to wrap. I'll take these over to the register and start tallying up your total."

"I'm almost done here and then I'll grab Bright, if I can pull him away, and we'll help wrap."

"Sounds wonderful." He hurried off towards his wife at the counter and Mary could hear them banter back and forth about such a Christmas miracle for the children on the angel tree. She was glad she could help fulfill a few wishes. She'd explain her extra charges to her mother, though she doubted her mother would care. Anything for the sake of the big party.

"Alright, I've found twenty-five more gifts." Bright pushed one cart and pulled another behind him.

"Looks like you've a bounty there, Mr. Smith."

"Man, I've had more fun looking and playing with all these toys, like a kid in a candy store." His boisterous laugh had her giggling. "You done?"

"I think so." She eyed her cart. "I would spend all day in here if I could."

"Likewise."

They pushed their carts to the front of the store to an awaiting Mr. Destin. Mrs. Destin was well underway wrapping the angel tree gifts with an expert's touch. As Mr. Destin finalized Mary's transaction, his eyes misted over when he read the total to her and accepted her credit card as payment. The elderly couple, emotional over such a gift and transaction for their business, thanked her profusely for her generosity. Uncomfortable with the praise, Mary fidgeted, until she felt Bright's hand rub a small, comforting circle in the middle of her back. A crackle of a spark ignited her insides at his touch, and she looked up to find him smiling down at her. Something passed between them in that small moment, a sudden explosion of acknowledgment in the midst of silent perusal.

Before she felt herself give into her emotions, Mary quickly turned her attention back to the Destins and helped Mr. Destin bag up the toys that would be leaving with her and Bright.

::

Mary closed the trunk on her car as another attendant rushed to her side to gather the bags of toys from her hands. Bright relinquished his as well as they were led into the Rutherford family home. He'd never been inside, and he felt a slight sense of awkwardness when he walked into the mansion with its polished floors and gleaming chandeliers. He followed the crowd as everyone climbed the winding staircase to the second floor and towards a door on the right. He entered to find a large suite.

A king-sized bed graced one side of the room, complete with four-posters and sheer canopy drapes. A fireplace, lit and warming the room as the bags of toys were placed on the luxuriously plush rug in front of it, crackled softly. A couch, loveseat, and deep-set chair nestled around the fireplace, and a television resting above the mantle was set to a blank screen playing only Christmas melodies. This was Mary's room. There were no personal mementos. No photographs. Only various portraits from artists unknown to him. The space was warm but lacked a personal touch.

Sighing, Mary plopped onto the couch and grinned at the pile of toys before her. "Have a seat."

He eyed their haul, which looked more impressive amongst a barren room than it did in a crowded toy store.

"They'll be bringing the wrapping paper and ribbons up soon. Want to stay and wrap presents? Or do you need to get back to Nonnie's?"

"I can stay for a bit." He slid to the floor and began unbagging some of the toys. "This is a good space to work on this."

"I'll have them bring up some food too. I'm starving." She walked to the phone and called down to the kitchen.

When she walked back towards the gifts, he looked up at her. "Is this your room?"

"Yep."

"As in, you grew up in this room?"

"Yes." She looked at him curiously.

"Wow." He glanced around again but when his gaze fell upon her, he realized she was embarrassed. "Must have been neat having such a big room as a kid."

She shrugged, not responding as she reached for the first bag of toys while attendants rushed in wrapping paper, tape, scissors, and ribbons and set them to the side at Mary's request.

Realizing he'd made her feel uncomfortable, he sobered. "Listen, Mary," he began, his voice turning serious. "I have a confession to make."

She eyed him curiously as she waited to hear what he could possibly say.

"I'm terrible at wrapping presents."

Her face relaxed into a warm glow as she smiled and laughed. "Trust me, I'm not awesome at it either. We'll struggle together. How about that?"

"Deal." He handed her a roll of wrapping paper before taking his own. Several failed attempts at wrapping a basketball had him tossing it to Mary to try.

"Note to self," she said. "Gift bags. We should have bought some gift bags." She held up the deformed package, the round ball roughly wrapped with a gaudy bow stuck to the top. "Lucky kid."

He laughed. "It's the thought that counts, right?"

She rolled her eyes. "My mom would flip if she saw this under her perfect trees. I'll set it aside and have one of the staff wrap it. They're better at this than I am. They've had more practice."

"Can I ask you something?"

"Sure." She reached for a puzzle box, opting for something simple, and began wrapping it.

"What was it like growing up with a house full of staff members and personal attendants?" He watched as her hands paused a moment before she looked at him. He could tell she was trying to decide whether or not to tell him the truth.

"Lonely," she said, her eyes serious. "You'd think with a house full of people it wouldn't be, but it was."

"I'm so sorry, Mary."

"Don't be. I can't complain. I was well taken care of. I never went without."

"Having our physical needs met is only part of growing up."

"My parents are good people; they were just busy."

"I don't doubt they're good people. They made you."

She looked back to her present and continued wrapping. "I had friends." She looked up again. "A few. And Nonnie." She smiled warmly, speaking of his grandmother. "I count myself fortunate."

Bright nodded in understanding. "I look around here and can't help but remember how intimidated I was by this place as a kid. I thought you must have had it made living in such a fancy house."

"Meanwhile, I was jealous of the fact you had a grandmother as awesome as Nonnie."

"Funny how things seem from a kid's perspective."

Mary sighed and leaned her back against the couch, her legs crossed beneath her as she set her package aside. "Want to know something else I envied?"

"What's that?" He looked down at his present and taped the folded paper into place.

"The kids in the Christmas parade. I always wondered what it would be like to be in the parade."

"But your parents' company has a float every year. You're telling me you never got to ride it?"

She shook her head.

Bright sat back stunned. "No way."

She bit back a smirk at his apparent bewilderment.

"Really?" he asked again.

"Really," she confirmed.

"But— you're— Wow. I don't know what to say, except that stinks. Wait—" He pointed at her. "Weren't you part of Student Council? Didn't they have a float?"

She nodded. "Yes, but only for the officers. I wasn't an officer."

"Oh come on!" He threw up his hands. "Seriously?"

She chuckled. "Seriously."

"Mary Rutherford, we are getting you on a float this year."

She laughed. "That's okay."

"No. We're doing it. You have to."

"And why is that?"

He waved his hands around at all the gifts. "Because look at what you're doing here. This deserves to be celebrated."

"That's not why I'm doing it."

"I know, but you deserve to be on a float."

She laughed. "And which float would I ride on?"

"R&S?"

She shook her head. "I'm afraid that is reserved for my parents."

He snapped his fingers. "I know exactly which one."

She raised her brow.

He pulled out his cell phone. "Mr. Destin? This is Brighten Smith. No, no, everything is great with the toys." He grinned at Mary as she shook her head and went back to wrapping. "I had a thought. Don't you have a Christmas parade float this year?" Silence hung for a moment. "Well, I wanted to run something by you. Could we possibly have Mary Rutherford ride on the float?"

Mary rose to her feet and walked to the door of her room and opened it to find her father standing on the other side.

"She's never been on a float," Bright explained. "And I'm wanting her to experience that... Perfect. I think that's a great idea. I'll let her know. Thank you, Mr. Destin." He hung up and turned at the sound of Mr. Rutherford's voice and stood to his feet.

Rowan looked to him in surprise. "I didn't realize you had company."

Mary pointed to the gifts. "Bright helped me shop for toys and is helping wrap them up."

"Wonderful." Rowan extended his hand. "Brighten Smith?"

"Yes sir."

"Nice to see you. I think the last time I saw you was when Ransforth lost the big game to Sanders. I blame you."

Bright chuckled as he rubbed his chin. "You wouldn't be the first."

Rowan grinned. "Having our star player on crutches on the sidelines was definitely a blow. But we all lived and moved on, didn't we?"

"Yes sir. We sure did."

"Thank you for helping Mary with her responsibilities."

"It's a pleasure. I've enjoyed catching up with her." Bright rested a hand at the small of Mary's back as her father eyed the gifts strewn about the floor.

"I'm glad." Rowan smiled politely as he turned his attention back to his daughter. "Your mother and I would like a word with you after dinner."

"Of course." Mary nodded as she closed the door behind her dad.

"Is he upset I'm here?" Bright asked.

"No, that's his normal self." Mary waved a nonchalant hand at the door. "I'm sure my mom is just wanting to know how much I've knocked off the family to-do list."

"Well, wrapping these gifts could take us hours yet. You want me to come back tomorrow to help since it is almost dinner time?"

She shook her head. "How about dinner? My treat."

He studied her a moment. Mary had grown into a beautiful woman. Dark eyes, gorgeous hair, soft face. He'd be a fool to turn her down, but he also didn't want her to miss the family meeting with her parents.

"Come on. You've earned it." She grinned as she reached for her purse and slipped it on her shoulder.

"Alright, I give in. But didn't you call to have dinner brought up here?"

She shrugged and reached for the phone on the small table by the door. Calling down to the kitchen and cancelling her request took seconds. She looked at him expectantly.

"Lead the way, Mary." He followed her down the winding staircase. Her mother stood at the base, her arms crossed, one hand fisted beneath her chin as she surveyed the decorations on the trees flanking each side of the stairs.

She looked up and followed them with her gaze. "Mary." She flashed what Bright assumed was her go-to smile for strangers and waited for introductions.

"Mom, you remember Brighten Smith from high school?"

"Ah, yes. Nonnie's grandson. This is who you hired for the catering, is it not?"

"Yes."

"I see." Molly extended her perfectly polished hand towards him. "I hope you are as good as Mary says you are, Mr. Smith."

"It's Bright," he corrected. "And I believe I will be, ma'am."

"Confident." Molly's brow quirked. "I like it." She slipped her hands to her waist and growled. "No, no, no," she scolded, stepping around them. "Titus, the ornaments are to alternate. In what world would three silver balls be hung next to one another when there's also blue and purple? Try again."

Mary motioned for him to follow her outside and shut the door behind them.

"She takes the decorating seriously, doesn't she?"

"You have no idea." Mary motioned to her car and Bright hopped inside to a warm interior, noting the attendant who waited beside Mary's door to open it for her. She slid behind the wheel and pulled around the circular drive towards the iron gates. When they reached the highway, she sighed and her shoulders immediately relaxed. He couldn't imagine living in such glamour and beauty but feeling as if you could never relax. He thought of her as a child in her room, the spacious suite a child's dream room in size, but empty of what he felt mattered most: joy. He wondered if Mary experienced much joy as a child. Her parents seemed kind, but aloof, and despite his family's incessant need to pry into his personal life, or hover over him at holidays, or even to call him one too many times during the day, he would take his family lifestyle over Mary's any day.

"I feel you staring at me." Mary cast a glance his way.

"Just wondering what it was like for you as a kid."

Her fingers flexed on the steering wheel. "It was okay."

"Just okay?"

"Just okay."

He watched her another moment before turning his attention back to the road ahead of them. He was determined to make this Christmas more than okay for Mary. While she was in town, he was going to make it the holiday to remember.

« CHAPTER FIVE »

"I can't eat another bite." Mary held her stomach as she nudged her empty plate towards the center of the table. "Lasagna is my favorite."

"It's pretty delicious." Bright looked out the window. "I almost forgot."

"What?"

He pointed towards the town square. "I bet Nonnie is out there decorating."

"We should help," Mary suggested. "I've kidnapped you all day to help me, it's only fair I return the favor."

"Alright. I guess we can reschedule our movie night. Nonnie will appreciate it for sure. Especially since we are decorating the focal point." Bright outstretched his arms. "Huge responsibility around here, so it seems."

Mary laughed. "I imagine it is. And what movie night?"

"I told you I was going to take you to see that action figure movie."

"Ah." She laughed as he held the door to the restaurant open and they stepped outside and crossed the street.

Nonnie welcomed them with her warm smile and enthusiasm. "I was wondering if you were going to show up." She nudged a handful of twinkle lights into Bright's hands. "I want the columns wrapped."

"Yes ma'am." Bright saluted and cast a grin Mary's way as he rushed to do Nonnie's bidding.

"And me?" Mary asked.

"You can help me drape the fabric. We're creating the spot where Santa will sit and visit with the children."

"Fun." Mary smiled as she lifted the fabric over the open beams to create a red and green backdrop for Santa's chair to sit in front of. Nonnie hung tinsel and snowflakes that descended from the beams as well. Bright plugged in the lights and the small space illuminated, providing extra light to their work in progress.

"Wonderful." Nonnie nodded in approval at the wrapping of the first column. "Keep going. We're going to light this gazebo up like a Christmas tree."

"You're well on your way—"

"Mary, can you hand me that other roll of lights?" Bright, standing on a ladder, peered down through his outstretched arms as he held his current string of lights in place. Mary hopped to it and quickly began unraveling the next row of lights just enough for him to plug them into his row. She helped him by wrapping the lights around the pole and handing them to him. They swapped the lights back and forth until he reached the bottom step of the ladder and accepted the last of the row to finish wrapping it to the floor. Mary knelt beside him to hold the last of the line so he could staple them into place. "Done." He glanced at her, her eyes focused on the pole, the soft light reflecting beautifully off her creamy complexion. She turned and caught him staring at her. She didn't flush this time, but instead offered a brief smile before he extended his hand to help her to her feet.

"You two tackle the rest of the poles," Nonnie ordered as she shifted the Christmas tree to the side of Santa's large wooden chair. "I'm going to decorate this tree."

"You're so good at decorating trees. I should have hired you to decorate the ones at my house."

Nonnie patted Mary's arm in thanks. "I've seen photos of those trees. I'm not sure if I could stand on a ladder long enough to reach that high." She chuckled as Bright climbed the ladder again and began freshly winding the next column. Mary watched as he expertly wound the lights and waited for him to ask for the next roll and her help. She liked Bright. He'd always been friendly in high school, but he'd grown into a thoughtful man. And handsome. Granted he'd always been good looking, but there was a bit of seasoning to him now. Life had sprinkled her mark on him, and he'd matured into a savory dish of confidence, kindness, and dreaminess. A dangerous combination.

"You good down there?" His voice broke Mary's trance and she rushed forward to hand him the plug for the next roll of lights. "Where'd you go?" He laughed as she shook her head to focus.

"I was lost in the moment."

"Twinkle lights do have a way of bringing out the fun of Christmas. As soon as they go up all over town, it's like I'm infected by the holiday spirit. Christmas season has officially started then."

"Right," Mary replied, though the holiday spirit was the farthest thing from her mind. Nonnie winked at her, which only embarrassed her further. Bright climbed down the ladder and she handed him the rest of the roll of lights. "You know, I'm sorry, but I just remembered I need to take care of something."

Her abruptness surprised him, she could tell, but Bright was too polite to question her. She brushed her cold hands on her pant legs before stuffing them into her coat pockets. "Thanks for helping me today."

Still confused as to her sudden change in attitude, Bright draped the lights on one of the ladder steps. "No problem. Is something wrong?"

"No. Not at all. I just... have to go. I'll touch base with you about the catering in a couple of days." She turned and gave Nonnie an apologetic smile. "Night, Nonnie."

"Good night, sweetie."

Mary rushed away and back across the street to her car, leaving a bewildered Bright standing beneath the twinkling lights.

::

"Stop pacing," Nonnie warned, as she took a small bite of the mac and cheese Bright had prepared. "This is perfect."

"You think so?"

"Yes. Absolutely divine."

"Good. Then that's the recipe I'll go with for the party." He reached for his cell phone on the counter and glanced at the screen.

"Still no word from Mary?" Nonnie rested her hand on his forearm.

"Um, no." Bright slid it into his pocket and shrugged as if not bothered by Mary's lack of communication.

Nonnie nudged him with her hand. "You can't fool me, Brighten. I can see you enjoy spending time with her."

Bright walked towards his recipes that were scattered about the small wooden table in the back of Nonnie's shop and rummaged through the sheets of paper until he found the one he was searching for. He held it up. "Wagon wheel carrots."

"Are you making a sampler platter for her?"

"Yes. I want her to be able to taste everything before we finalize all the dishes."

"She trusts you," Nonnie began. "I don't think you need to create every single dish for her prior to the party."

"I'm not a caterer, Nonnie. Heck, I'm not even a chef or cook or baker or anything. I don't want to screw this up for her."

Nonnie tilted her head as she watched him hustle around her kitchen. "Then why did you commit to such a task? Why go through all this trouble for a woman you barely know?"

"Because she needed someone."

"She would have found a caterer sooner or later."

"Yeah, but—"

Nonnie's brow rose and he bit off the last of his remark. "Nevermind. That doesn't matter now. I'm the caterer and I want the dishes I prepare to be the best she's had—" He paused a moment to correct himself. "The best *they've* had in a long time."

His phone rang and he hurriedly fetched it out of his pocket, only to his disappointment it was his sister instead of Mary. "Hey, Grace," he greeted. "I can't today, sorry. I'm working on the R&S Distributions Christmas party menu. I know, I'm already receiving the lecture from Nonnie." He covered the mouthpiece and whispered towards his grandmother. "She thinks I'm in over my head too." He turned his focus back to the phone. "Yeah, I'll be sure to let Mary know. Yes, I promise to stress the fact I'm a complete fool. Thanks." He smirked as he hung up. "Everyone seems to think I'm completely crazy."

"Oh, we don't think you're crazy." Nonnie bustled past him towards the front of her shop. "Just a little smitten."

"What?" He looked to his grandmother in surprise.

"With Mary," Nonnie supplied. "You're smitten with Mary," she repeated. "Don't be so shy about it."

"But how would Grace know anything about it?" He waved his hands as if to rid the topic from the room. "Wait, I'm not saying I am smitten. I'm just— what— how— how did Grace even know of my working with Mary?"

"I may have let it slip the other night after the gazebo incident."

"What incident?" Bright asked.

Nonnie giggled. "Bright... be *bright* for a moment and use that noggin of yours. Clearly you and Mary had a moment that made her nervous and scurry off."

"She had something to see to."

"Feathers!" Nonnie waved away the excuse. "That girl realized she liked you and got scared. That is what sent her runnin'."

"This is ridiculous." Bright threw up his hands and then rested them on his hips. "That's not true. She has a lot on her plate. As do I, so I don't need any of this matchmaking business interfering with the work I've got to get done for the party. I also don't want you making Mary feel uncomfortable with these notions of yours."

"Oh, I won't. That girl is delicate when it comes to matters of the heart. I know her better than most."

Bright blew a frustrated breath at Nonnie still continuing her descriptions of heart matters and attractions. Thankfully, his phone buzzed again, and despite the brief annoyance that flashed at Mary's name on the screen, he also could not ignore the small jump in his chest as well. "Mary," he greeted warmly. "I was just thinking about y—" He cleared his throat at Nonnie's knowing smile. "Thinking of *calling* you," he corrected. "Yes, I'm at Nonnie's, come on by." He hung up and pointed a finger at his giddy grandmother. "Behave, Nonnie." He suppressed a smile and walked to the main counter as Mary stepped through the door, the Christmas carols ringing as she did so. She looked up and smiled, and again he felt that small jolt in his chest. She was just here for the holidays, he reminded himself. A brief trip home to help her parents pull off their annual party and then she'd be gone again. Granted, Landisburg was only a couple of hours away. Not too far, as far as long-distance relationships go.

Her fingers snapped in front of his face and had him blinking and kicking himself for the rabbit trail his mind had begun to follow. "Earth to Bright."

"Sorry. Hey. I'm here."

She laughed. "Obviously. You okay? I'm not wearing you out, am I?"

"No. Not at all. I've been creating all kinds of great food back there for you to sample."

"Is that so?"

"Yep. Let me go get what I have."

She reached out and placed a hand on his arm. "I can't stay. Not right this moment." She grimaced. "I'm sorry. I just wanted to swing by and give you this." She extended an embossed envelope his direction, the swirly handwriting a formal invitation to the R&S Distribution Christmas Gala, as it read across the front.

"Oh." He ran a finger over his name on the front. "Looks nice."

"Look at the invitation."

He opened the envelope and pulled out the small slip of cardstock.

She pointed towards the bottom and smiled, her eyes bright, as she studied his reaction to the mention of a toy drive benefiting local charities. "Your idea coming to fruition." Proudly, she patted him on the arm. "What do you think?"

"Looks good." He tapped it against the palm of his hand. "Thanks for bringing it by."

"You're welcome." She beamed as she shouldered her purse once again. "I've got to go. I've got an appointment with my mother at a dress shop in Sheraton."

"A new dress for the big night, huh?"

"Always." Mary rolled her eyes.

"Hey, call me when you're back in town this evening. You owe me a movie night, remember?"

Her cheeks flushed as Nonnie walked into the room and heard the last snippet of his question. "Um, sure. I'll... call you." Shyly, she ducked out of the store and hurried to her car, her red scarf getting caught in her door when she closed it. She quickly opened the door one more time and tugged it inside before backing out of the parking spot.

"Movie night?" Nonnie asked.

Bright held up his hand to hold back any of Nonnie's further comments. All he heard was her soft giggle, which made him smile as he made his way back to the kitchen.

::

"Well, what did you think?" Bright steered his truck down the long drive leading to the entrance of Mary's house. Attendants waited at the door as they pulled to a stop.

"I think the action figure toys were a good buy." Grinning, she reached for her purse.

He laughed. "Good."

Her door opened and an attendant stood to the side, hand on the door handle as he waited for her to climb out of the truck. "Thank you," she told the man. She stepped out and Bright exited the truck as well, rounding the hood to talk with her a bit longer. He slipped his hands into his pant pockets, his jacket still tossed in the backseat and the winter chill piercing through his sweater.

"I had fun. Thanks for taking me." Mary nodded towards the attendant and the man dismissed himself by slipping quietly back into the house, though the door remained ajar.

"Has Mr. Destin called you about the parade yet?" Bright rested his back against his truck and propped one foot on his bumper.

"Yeah, so about that..." Mary crossed her arms and stepped towards him. She looked up at him, a gleam in her eye. "Apparently I have to dress up in an angel costume."

His lips twitched.

"Which means you have to dress up to."

"I'm not going to be on the float. Just you," he pointed out.

"Actually, that's not true." She held up her finger and grinned. "After I tossed out an idea, Mr. Destin thought it a wonderful plan to have you on board as well."

"And what plan is that?" Bright asked.

"Well, Mr. Destin is going to be Santa Claus, as he always is, Mrs. Destin his Mrs. But it just wouldn't be the same if they didn't have an elf."

Bright shook his head as she gleefully tugged on his crossed arms and laughed.

"A bearded elf. I'm sure that won't freak the kids out."

She squeezed his hand and spun in a circle. "You'll be tossing out candy, they won't care what you look like."

"So, I now have to find an elf costume, is that what you're saying?"

"Mrs. Destin assured me she had one."

Bright groaned and it only encouraged Mary's mirth. He finally laughed. "Fine. I'll do it. But only because it's your first time on a Christmas float. This is not to be an annual tradition."

"I thought you liked traditions."

He nudged her away and towards her front door. "You're trouble, Mary Rutherford."

She stopped on the front step and watched as he stood in front of his truck, hands in his pockets, watching her. She liked him there. He wasn't intimidated by her house, the attendants, her name. He just stood there, confident and all smiles. Smiles aimed towards her.

Her face sobered a moment. "I'll be busy the next few days with party prep."

He listened and his eyes sobered.

"But I'll check in with you. And if you need me to answer any questions about the party, feel free to call or text me."

He walked towards her and stood a step below her. "And what if I want to call or text you about *non*-party business?"

Mary placed a cold hand to her flushed cheek at his insinuation, flabbergasted that Brighten Smith would ask such a thing. Realizing she'd yet to answer him, she looked up to find his patient eyes settled upon her face. "That'd be okay too... if you want."

"I do." He reached for her hand and squeezed it. "Have fun dress shopping with your mom." Releasing his grip, he slipped away and back towards his truck. She watched as his taillights disappeared up the drive before she walked inside.

Her father stood to the side of the door, his sudden appearance causing her to jump and place a hand over her heart. An amused smile crossed his face. "Mr. Smith on his way then?"

"Yes." Mary hid her embarrassment by unwrapping her scarf.

"He seems to have grown into a nice young man," Rowan Rutherford continued.

"Yes. Seems that way. Were you waiting up for me, Dad?" Mary chuckled softly at her own dad's embarrassment that he'd be caught doing such a thing.

"Not in the slightest. I saw you driving up and wanted to have a word with you."

"Alright."

He motioned for her to follow him into his study and closed the door. "Have a seat." He motioned to a stiff leather chair opposite his desk. The room smelled of lemon polish and subtle cigar smoke. She watched as her dad poured himself a small glass of whiskey and set the crystal decanter back on the silver tray to the left of his desk. He sighed as he sat.

"Everything okay, Dad?"

"Tired is all." He studied her a moment and took his first long sip, taking a moment to savor the taste. "You've done an excellent job preparing for the party."

"Thanks. I feel like we've got the ball rolling pretty well." She smiled as she sat her purse on the floor beside her feet.

"Mr. Smith have a menu planned?"

"Yes, we settled on it this morning."

"Good. Good." Rowan crossed his hands on his desk a moment before reaching towards a blank file folder and sliding it towards her.

Confused, Mary reached for it and opened it. Her eyebrows shot into her hairline. "What?"

"It's time, Mary."

"But—" She paused a moment to place a shaking hand over her mouth. "I never thought—"

"I know. And I'm sorry for that." Rowan reached for the folder and she all but tossed it at him as if it held the country's deepest secrets. "I'm offering it to you first. If you do not wish to take my position, I have a couple of in-house employees in mind. But you're a Rutherford, and I'd like to keep R&S Distribution in the family."

"You were always so adamant you didn't want me to work for the company. Why now?"

"I wanted you to have a life outside of Ransforth." Rowan held up his finger. "Something I never received, nor my father. We were expected to take over the business and it was all we were allowed to think about from age eleven until manhood. I didn't want that for you. I wanted you to have the freedom to do what you like."

"Then why now?"

"Because you've proven you're a successful businesswoman. You've accomplished much in your time with Donning's Footwear."

"But to take over the entire distribution center? I'm not ready for that."

"Of course you're not completely ready," Rowan replied. "But you will be. If you come to work with me, I can teach you what you need to know. With your background already in distribution, there's not much else you would need to learn."

"*With* you, not *for* you?"

"Exactly. You will enter into the company as my replacement. I will only stay on for as long as you need me to. The position is yours if you want it. I know it's much to consider, especially since it would require your relocation back to Ransforth."

"Right." She reached for the folder again and looked over his formal offer. Not only would she be given the company and the salary, but the deed to the house was beneath the forms. She held it up. "And this?"

"All it needs is your signature."

"But you and Mom."

"Will remain here as long as we want. That's in one of the clauses." He pointed his finger for her to read further down. "But it's only natural that it pass to you. We originally had everything settled in our estate planning, but I figured we might as well take care of it now. As long as you're okay with having us around for a bit."

"It's your house, of course you can stay here."

He leaned back in his chair and sipped on his drink as he watched her look over the papers.

"You don't have to answer now. Take your time. I know you've built a life in Landisburg, and just because you are my daughter and only heir, that does not mean you *have* to take the offer. I don't want you to feel pressured, Mary."

"But if I don't take it, it won't be in the family anymore."

"Yes, it will. It will just have someone else leading the helm."

She never thought her father would relinquish the company to her. Not in a million years. It had always been stressed that it wouldn't. So now, here she sat, completely dumbfounded that her dad was all but handing it to her on a silver platter. Speechless, mummified, and out of sorts, Mary closed the folder. "I'll think on it. When would you like my answer?"

"How about Christmas day? That gives you several weeks to see if you would like to stay here in Ransforth, and it also gives you an opportunity to mingle with the employees at the party on Christmas Eve."

"Alright." She stood and extended her hand. Her dad's brow etched slightly up his forehead, but he shook her hand in a firm deal. "I'll let you know Christmas day, then. Thanks, Dad."

She slipped out of his office and up the stairs to her suite. When she closed her door, she ran and launched herself on the oversized bed with a sigh. Rolling over, she stared at the canopied overhangs and pondered what her life would look like if she accepted his offer. She loved her job at Donning's Footwear, but she'd admit she didn't have much of a life outside of work. In Ransforth, she'd at least have her parents around... though she'd admit that'd never mattered much to her. Perhaps this was her dad's way of nurturing more of a relationship between them. If she turned it down, she may miss out on special time with her parents. However, she also held a bit of resentment towards them there as well. They've had her whole life to reach out to her, to try and create a relationship with her but they chose not to. She was always in the background, pawned off on a nanny or staff member. She'd be closer to Nonnie. She had to admit that she'd enjoy more visits with the Smith family matriarch. She loved Nonnie. And then there was Bright. She had at least one friend in Ransforth. She felt a flutter in her stomach at the thought of Bright standing out front of her house. A giddiness she hadn't felt before trembled up her spine as she thought of getting to know him better. Odd how someone she knew in high school could swoop back into her life and have her feeling this way. But he was just a friend, a business colleague, really. He was her caterer, nothing more, and she needed to remember that. The Christmas party was now a way for her to show the employees of R&S Distribution that she was ready to take the lead. She needed to focus on making it a success. Especially *if* she decided to take her dad's offer. *If.*

« CHAPTER SIX »

Nonnie rushed about the small kitchen space and wiped down a countertop as Bright pulled another sheet pan of cookies out of the oven. He held the pan high into the air so Nonnie could pass beneath him towards the other end of the room. "This kitchen was not made for a caterer." She ducked back under his arm and back towards her section of the counter. She removed the chocolate cookies from the pan and placed them on a cooling rack. She then began dusting them with confectioner's sugar as Bright was already sliding in the next tray.

"Thanks again for helping me, Nonnie."

"If I have the time, I will. And right now, I have the time." She smiled up at him. "You're doing a wonderful job so far. Mary will be proud and thankful."

"This is the last of the cookies. Then I'll start on pie crusts for all the mini pies." He held up the small foil pans Mary had ordered, the sight of 400 of the small holders intimidating him more and more by the second. But when he looked at what all he'd accomplished so far with the cookies, he knew he could do it. "I never thought I'd be baking cookies and pies for a living."

"You aren't," Nonnie reminded him. "You're helping out a friend."

"True, but I have yet to do much with my graphic design business since I moved here."

"There's plenty of time for that," Nonnie reminded him.

"I know." Bright paused a moment and ran a hand over his face.

"Take a deep breath." Nonnie chuckled.

Bright did as he was told.

"Feel better?"

"A little."

"Any word from Mary?"

"Not for a few days. Other than her dropping these off to me." He pointed at all the pans that were stacked above Nonnie's cabinets. "She left a note saying she would have chafing dishes on the tables to keep the food heated. I will admit I had to do an internet search to even know what chafing dishes were."

Nonnie giggled and rested a hand on his arm. "You're doing wonderful, sweetie. Just keep your focus on food preparation and let Mary handle presentation."

A Christmas tune jingled and Nonnie wound her way out of the kitchen to the front of the shop. "We were just talking about you."

Relief swamped over Bright as he realized it had to be Mary. He needed her assurance that he was on the right path. He didn't want her to see him floundering under the pressure, so he plastered a smile on his face when she entered the kitchen. She grinned. "Smells pretty incredible in here."

"Thanks. We are on the last batch of cookies."

"Wow, progress." She reached for one cooling on the rack and took a bite. Her face contorted and she forced herself to swallow.

"Is something wrong?"

"Um…" she walked over to the sink and filled a cup with water and took a long drink. "It's interesting."

"It's chocolate. It can't be that interesting." He snatched the cookie from her hand and bit into it. He immediately spit into the trash can and growled in frustration as he emptied the freezer containers of the same batch into the trash. "I must have been distracted. The first batch tastes fine."

He reached into another container and handed her a cookie. She took a bite and nodded. "Much better. Best taste one from each batch." She winked at him as he ran a hand over the back of his neck. "I brought more pans. I'm assuming you'll bake and cook everything in pans, and we'll transfer to the serving dishes once you arrive."

"That works for me."

"You feeling okay?"

"I'm good. Just… trying not to feel overwhelmed."

"You're doing fantastic. Look at the ground you've covered. And we still have a week and a half before the party."

"And I still have 400 mini pies to make, six spiral hams, carrots, asparagus, mac and cheese, deviled eggs, dressing, potatoes… the list goes on and on and on."

Worry crossed her face.

"I can handle it," he reassured her. "I'm just feeling the pressure today."

"Bright—"

"No, I've got this. Don't worry. I don't want you to lose faith in me. I shouldn't have said anything. It's coming together."

"Well, I will be free after five today. I can come by and help if you want?"

"That'd be great. I planned to start on the pies after this."

"Great. I'll bring dinner." She snatched another cookie out of the container and headed for the door.

"Stop stealing my progress," Bright called after her. He heard a brief laugh as she exited. He inhaled a deep breath, already feeling better and feeling grateful she was willing to come help him.

Nonnie ducked back into the kitchen and cast a pitying glance at the cookies in the trash can.

"A minor mishap."

"Oh, Brighten." Nonnie gave him a reassuring hug.

"I'm going to whip up the replacement batch and then *that* will be the last batch of cookies. If you are still willing to help me out, I would appreciate you starting on pie crusts for these." He handed her the small pie pans.

"Of course. I have the perfect tool for this as well." She reached into one of the cupboards and withdrew a glass drinking cup. "The mouth of this cup is the perfect size for cutting out the crusts for the pans."

"Good trick."

Nonnie tapped her temple and began grabbing ingredients and dusting the counter with flour.

"By the time you finish those cookies, you'll have an hour or so before Mary returns. Which pies do you plan on baking first?"

"Chocolate. The filling takes time, so if I can knock out the most difficult ones first, then the rest shouldn't take too much time."

Nonnie didn't mutter a word.

"You don't like that plan?"

"Chocolate is one of the easiest, sweetie. I'd start with your chess pies. The filling takes a little longer to bake than a chocolate pie."

"Alright, I'll start with chess. Then chocolate."

"Yes, one of you can be filling the chess pies while the other works on cooking the chocolate filling."

They worked in tandem with one another for the next couple of hours, Nonnie darting in and out of the kitchen to wait on her own customers as they came into the shop to purchase a number of her own delectable treats. By the time Mary walked into the kitchen, her purse strung over her shoulder, her hair disheveled from the beanie she'd worn most of the day, the cookies were complete and stored away and the mini pie shells rested on any open and available surface.

"Wow. You two have been busy."

Nonnie washed her hands. "And with your arrival, that ends my shift." She lightly brushed a kiss over Bright's cheek. "We have all the pie crusts prepared for the first hundred."

"And I've got the filling ready to pour." Bright pointed to several large measuring bowls.

Nonnie handed Mary an apron. "Good luck, you two." She grabbed Bright's keys off the counter and left through the back of the shop, eager to give them time alone.

Mary quickly pulled her hair back into a perky ponytail and washed her hands. "Alright, so I'll start filling?"

"Yes, if you don't mind. I'm going ahead and starting on the chocolate filling."

"Think we can get them all cooked tonight?"

"All 400?" He shook his head. "Let's aim for two hundred. Two different kinds."

"Got it. How many trays can bake at the same time?"

"Four. Twenty-five per tray."

"Perfect, so we can slip all the same flavor in at one time."

"That's the idea."

She slowly began to pour the batter into the pie shells while he stirred the cocoa into the butter on the stovetop.

"How was your day?" he asked.

"Good. I was able to work on the table set up in the dining hall. I figured we'd put the main dishes in there and have a dessert room in the parlor where the focal tree is. Line tables up along the windows." She moved her hand in the air as if shaping the display for him to visualize. "My mother is decorating around and on them as we speak. She specifically asked for the role of "making the tables." And surprisingly, she wasn't appalled at my menu ideas."

"I'm glad."

"I also started thinking, if you need to, you can use the kitchen at the house for food preparation. You'd have more space to work with and it would familiarize you with the area for the night of the party." Mary used a rubber spatula to scrape the last of the batter into the last pie shell.

"I'll think about it. Right now, I feel more comfortable and less intimidated here."

"I get that. It was just a suggestion."

"I appreciate it." He slipped her completed trays off the counter and walked them one by one to the oven. He set a timer as he closed the door and felt himself relax a smidgen more as one more item was marked off his list.

"Do I need to make pie crust for the next hundred?" Mary asked.

"Nope. Already done. Nonnie whipped together all the crusts we'll need. She wrapped the dough and it's resting in the fridge." He pointed to the large commercial sized refrigerator and Mary opened to find neatly stacked packages of prepared dough.

"Awesome."

"Yeah, just use that cup there to cut the size."

"How very crafty of you." Mary grinned as she used the mouth of the glass to cut a perfect circle of dough.

"Nonnie's idea."

"She seems to be way ahead of us."

"Always." Bright walked towards her and placed an empty tray on the counter next to her work area so she could place the pie shells on the pan to prepare them for baking.

"Thanks." She placed three mini pies on the pan as she continued to cut and watched as he went back to the stovetop to stir his chocolate filling. "So, something big happened the other day after our movie night."

His brows rose. "Oh?"

She directed her attention to her task of cutting the dough, her eyes purposely avoiding him. A strand of hair slipped from her ponytail and teased the side of her face, but she didn't stop her progress. "My dad offered me the company."

"R&S?"

She looked up then and found him standing closer to her, his back leaning against the countertop, arms crossed over his chest giving her his full attention. He looked at her busy hands as she continued to cut out the circle shaped pie crusts. "And?" he asked.

"I'm to give him my decision on Christmas Day."

"Wow." Bright exhaled a heavy breath. "That's a big deal."

"Yeah. I never thought this was even in the cards. Sort of took me by surprise, you know?"

He nodded. "I imagine it did. Any idea what you're going to do? Have you made a decision?"

She shook her head. "Not yet. There's much to consider. One, I love my job in Landisburg, and two, I'm not sure if I want to move back to Ransforth. I just never envisioned my life here after I left."

He listened and didn't interrupt because he knew part of her sharing this with him was her sorting it out for herself.

"But then I think about it being a family business and I don't want to disappoint my dad by not accepting it. I mean, I never even knew he was considering me."

"That must feel pretty good, right?"

"Yes and no." She looked up at him, her eyes worried about making the wrong choice. "Part of me is thrilled, and the other part of me is a tad bitter. I'm trying not to let that part take over. All these years, I assumed I was just cast aside and never going to live up to the Rutherford name because I wasn't a male heir to the business. And I was somewhat treated that way. But come to find out, my dad just wanted me to have a life. Why couldn't he just tell me that? Why did he make it seem like he didn't want me around?"

Bright rested a comforting hand on her arm, and she stopped cutting the pie dough. He tugged her floured hands away from the work and held them in his own. "I'm sure your dad was trying to navigate or figure out how to navigate along the way. I don't say this to defend what he did and has done, but only that maybe he was confused as to how to proceed with the business as well. Maybe he just didn't want the heavy burden of the business placed on your shoulders at such a young age."

"That's what he said." Her words sounded less convinced that that was her father's true purpose. "But it's hard to accept that reasoning when he barely even acknowledged me over the years. And that's not me being harsh or dramatic. I spent most of my childhood years secluded in my room or sent with a nanny. The only time I really saw my parents was at dinner, and even then, I was excused as soon as my plate was empty. He never once shared anything about the company with me. Not once. It seemed like a sigh of relief for everyone when I graduated high school and headed off to college. So, to hear him say he'd planned to give me the company all along comes as more than a surprise."

"I bet so."

"What would you do?" she asked.

His brows rose and he heaved in uncertainty. "It's a big decision. And I'm not the person to ask. I went off and tried a life in California and it didn't work out. I was thankful to have Ransforth to come back to. My family and I are close." He trailed off, realizing what he'd said.

"Yeah, I guess we are different in that regard." She reached for the glass again and began cutting crusts, but immediately set it back down. "Am I wrong to not just jump at the chance?"

"No. I think your dad would be worried if you did. He knows how big of a decision this is for you. I imagine he expects you to weigh the options."

"Added to this, if I do accept the position, then the Christmas party is my time to show the employees that I can handle the responsibility."

"No pressure." Bright's lips tilted and she rolled her eyes.

"Exactly." She gazed around the room at all the pies. "So we have to pull this off. It has to be the best annual party they've ever had."

"And *that* doesn't freak me out at all." His nervous chuckle had her eyes softening.

"You're doing great, Bright. And I can't do this without you. We're going to knock this out of the park together."

"Then I suggest," He tugged on the tie of her apron. "that we get busy. We've got a load of food to make, Mary Rutherford."

"That we do." Her smile relaxed and she slid her arms around his waist and squeezed. Surprised, he returned her hug. "Thanks, Bright."

The warm kitchen, flour dusted hands, and the sweet scent of cinnamon had Bright hugging Mary closer. He had to admit, it felt nice having her in his arms. On top of that, he felt her need for reassurance just as much as he needed, and the fact they could give that to one another made the moment sweeter. He felt her shoulders relax, and though he dreaded to let go, he released his hold and let her slip out of his arms and back towards her task at the counter.

« CHAPTER SEVEN »

"Y ou look absolutely angelic." Mrs. Destin, dressed in a bright red dress with crisp white apron adorned with candy canes, clasped her hands together and swooned over Mary. "I just knew that dress would be the perfect angel costume. Obviously, I had to make a few adjustments." She pointed to the cinched waist that brought the A-line flare to the shape of the dress. "But the lace is so delicate, almost like a snowflake. And I hope you don't mind, but I modified Brighten's outfit as well."

She motioned towards the door leading to the stockroom of the toy store. Mr. Destin stepped out, his white Santa beard hanging around his neck. He smiled and held the door open for Bright. Mary felt her breath catch as he walked out adjusting the sleeve to his solid white three-piece suit. He looked up and his lips split into a dazzling smile. "You look fantastic." He looked her up and down and she felt warmth follow his gaze.

"You do too. Not like any elf I've ever seen."

"You've seen an elf?" he asked playfully.

Mrs. Destin chortled. "We couldn't have one angel, so we decided on two." She placed a golden halo around Mary's head, sitting more like a flower crown than a halo, and she did the same for Bright.

"What's missing?" Mrs. Destin stepped back and eyed them with an artist's squint. She clapped her hands. "Oh yes, the wings." She hurried to the back room and came back with large widespread wings that slipped on like a backpack. She helped Mary slip her arms through the straps and then did the same for Bright.

The wings were a glossy sheer fabric imbedded with tiny sequins that gave them a touch of shimmer when turned towards the light. They were a far cry from the cardboard cut outs Mary remembered seeing in Christmas plays as a child. From afar, they almost looked real. Bright looked the part of fairy prince instead of angel, but Mary wasn't complaining. Bright gave her a thorough look over and nodded his approval. "I think you're the prettiest angel I've ever seen."

"You've seen an angel?" she quipped and had him laughing.

"No, but I imagine they do not hold a candle to you."

"I'm not sure about that, but thanks." She brushed her hands over the front of her dress. "I can't believe I let you talk me into this."

"You nervous?"

"Yes."

"Why?"

"Because the whole town goes to the parade."

"And?"

"And I've never had the whole town staring at me before, unlike you."

He grinned. "Those days are over for me, thankfully."

Mrs. Destin shuffled them out the door and towards the trailer that housed their massive float. The Destins, along with their employees, had outdone themselves with Christmas spirit. Santa's chair was ornately carved, though upon closer inspection, Mary noticed it was just glue drawn in intricate patterns, allowed to harden, and then spray-painted the same brown as the chair. *How industrious,* she thought. From the ground it looked like a real, wooden chair designed perfectly for Santa. She slipped out of her wings to fit into the van that would carry them to the parade float parking lot. When they arrived, she and Bright climbed out and helped one another with their wings yet again. She fluffed her hair and nervously wound her hands together as she waited for the Destins to climb into their spots on the float. Bright lifted himself up onto the float and extended his hand to help her up. She lifted her dress so as not to trip and accepted his assistance. Mrs. Destin positioned them at the back of the float under the arching sign that wished everyone a Merry Christmas, the tiered steps creating a rounded platform that looked as if they stood at the top of a tree. Bright continued to hold Mary's hand, and the warmth of his grip not only helped in keeping her body temperature up in the cold weather, but also settled her nerves.

A man raised a bar on the back of the trailer to give them something to hold on to and shot a thumbs up at the driver.

"Ready?" Bright asked, his voice near her ear.

She shivered, blaming the cold, but she knew better. She smiled up at him. "I think so."

"I like your sleeves." Bright ran a finger down one of the long bell sleeves. "Makes you look even more whimsical."

The trailer jerked and Mary stumbled towards Bright. "Steady, Rutherford." He released her hand and slid his to the small of her back for support. The slow crawl was less intimidating as they followed the floats in front of them. Baskets of candy were on either side of them to throw to all the children that would line the streets. They rounded the curve onto Main Street and the cheers and screaming began as people applauded the high school students that graced various floats. Candy started flying.

"Bright! Bright!" A loud group chanted his name and he laughed when he saw his family. He tapped Mary's arm and she turned to find Nonnie waving enthusiastically at them, Bright's nieces and nephews yelling for candy. She and Bright grabbed fistfuls and tossed it their direction. Grace, Bright's sister, held up her camera and snapped a photo of them on the float before they rolled onward.

"That will be in the family slideshow, I'm sure." Bright grinned as he tossed candy towards a crowd of kids waving their hands at them.

"It's not every day that Uncle Bright dresses up in a costume?" Mary asked.

"Not in the slightest. This is because of you, Mary Rutherford."

Gleeful, she flashed a smile at him before hearing her own name being called from the street. She and Bright glanced the direction of the yells and saw her parents waving at them. "What in the world?" Mary stood stunned as Bright waved and tossed a handful of candy to the kids in front of her parents. "Why are they not on the R&S float?" Mary asked.

"Maybe they didn't want to."

She waved at them, baffled that they stood amongst the rest of the townspeople, crowded along the side of the street. Her dad shot a thumbs up her direction before her attention needed to turn towards other members of the crowd and candy throwing.

Mrs. Destin turned their direction as the float came to a complete stop in the center of town and the high school marching band began playing Christmas carols and the cheerleaders and dance team danced a routine alongside them. As Santa, Mr. Destin stood and walked off the float to go shake hands with children who couldn't fathom Santa Claus in their midst and danced in excitement at his attention. Bright helped Mary down the steps of the float, and they proceeded to hand out candy to various impatient hands. Looking up, she noticed Bright walking back towards the float and hurried over. He hoisted her up the back just as the float began its onward progression, the two of them gripping the rail in hopes of steadying their feet at the shift underneath them. "You almost got left behind." Bright helped her situate her dress as they resumed their position as tree-topping angels. When she looked up to thank him, small flakes of snow began falling around them. She held her hands out as the soft downfall began to grow even heavier. A light dusting coated Bright's hair. She shivered as a cold breeze sliced through her costume and sent a jolt down her spine. "Uh oh." Bright pointed to the small heater set beside them, the machine no longer blowing a soft warmth in their direction. Her shoulders jittered as the cold seeped beneath her skin.

Teeth chattering, she crossed her arms and tucked her hands inside her billowing sleeves. "H-how m-much longer is the p-parade?"

His smile turned sympathetic. "At least a half hour."

The snow continued to fall, growing heavier by the minute. The bystanders loved the extra touch of Christmas novelty, but Mary was quickly growing miserable. Her toes had long since gone numb, and her fingers felt as if tiny spikes were poking into her skin. Bright grabbed her hands and rubbed them in his own. He cupped them around his mouth and blew warm breath over her fingers and rubbed them some more, but it didn't help. "Hold on, I have an idea." He stepped down to Mrs. Destins area and slid one of the heavy blankets off the back of one of the benches gracing the sides of the float. He hurried back to his position and started to drape it over Mary's shoulders, only to realize her wings prevented the blanket from covering her shoulders and back.

"I guess my a-angel days are o-over." She slipped out of her wings and Bright laid them to the side as he wrapped the blanket tightly around her and rubbed her arms. "A-are you n-not c-cold?"

"I am, but I have a jacket on at least. I don't know why I didn't think about bringing gloves."

"M-me either. T-they wouldn't h-have g-gone with my d-dress."

He grinned. "I will say, despite the blueish tint to your lips, the snow makes you look even more beautiful."

"Y-you think I'm b-beautiful?"

He paused in his attempt to warm her up and focused upon her face. His eyes turned serious. She shouldn't have asked the question. Now she'd made him feel uncomfortable when he was only being nice and complimentary. This was one of those moments she wished to be the old

Mary, the one who could easily blend into her surroundings and disappear.

"I do. Very much," he admitted.

She felt warmth ease its way back into her body as he stepped closer to her. Her heart raced as he leaned his head down towards hers. His lips were a breath from her own as she closed her eyes to await his kiss. A lurch had them both staggering and bumping into one another as the float screeched to a stop at the end of the parade, one final farewell from Santa and the marching band underway around them. Embarrassed, Mary gathered her dress and hurried down off the float to finish handing out candy and to do what she did best, disappear.

::

"I can't talk right now, Grace, I'm in over my head in glazed carrots at the moment." Bright finished emptying the foil pan's contents into one of the chafing dishes, an attendant intercepting the foil pan and carrying it away. He pointed to one of the other attendants and motioned towards the dressing. The woman immediately began transferring it to the corresponding trays as well. He wasn't used to having staff at his beck and call, but he was thankful for them. They rushed around completely calm as if working with a crazy man was their normal day-to-day routine. His sister's voice drifted through the line and had his attention snapping back to his phone. "Sure. Yes. I'll be there first thing in the morning, presents and all." He hung up, stuffing his phone in the front pocket of the apron Nonnie insisted he wear. It was professionally white and plain. He may have looked the part of caterer, but at the moment he was suffering from imposter syndrome as he attempted to not feel overwhelmed by all the busy bodies.

"Mr. Smith," A man in a server's suit entered the kitchen. "Ms. Mary wishes for you to meet her in the dining hall."

Bright wiped his hands on a dish towel and then hurried towards the table set up. He feared what he might find. *What if his food was a complete fail? What if people hated it? What if Mary's parents hated it and then grew frustrated with her for hiring him?* His swirling thoughts evaporated the moment he saw Mary standing in a silver, sequined top surrounded by crystal serving dishes. The stainless steel, the silver, and the crystal ricocheted light around the room and onto her dress and she sparkled. The dress was a sequined top that paired with a voluminous black satin skirt that brushed just above the floor. She looked stunning.

She held her hands out towards the tables. "What do you think?"

He diverted his gaze from gawking at her appearance to the serving tables, the decorative touches and display of dishes perfectly placed to create an inviting and gorgeous display.

"It looks amazing."

"All your hard work, Mr. Smith." She nudged his elbow with her own. "Not bad, hm?"

He ran a hand over the front of his apron as Mary's mother swept into the room in a pale blue dress that made her look like a snow queen. Her makeup, much like Mary's, was impeccable, and the two women looked like they belonged on the cover of a magazine rather than hosting a party in small town, USA. "Ah, Mr. Smith," Molly lightly touched his arm. "I want to thank you for pulling all of this together so beautifully. I will admit that when Mary first told me who she'd hired, I had my doubts. But this just looks wonderful."

"Thank you, ma'am. I hope you enjoy it."

"Enjoy it? I just had to go brush my teeth for the second time and reapply my lipstick because I've snuck two cookies already." She playfully swatted his arm. "Delicious." She looked proudly at Mary. "I knew you would come through, Mary. I had full faith."

"Thanks, Mom."

Molly lightly touched a hand to her styled hair. "Guests will be here any minute, Mary. Your father wants you at the door to greet everyone."

"I'll be there." Mary watched her mom leave and Bright patiently waited for her to return her attention to him.

"Anything else you need me for?" He asked.

She slipped her hands in his and squeezed them. "For a confidence boost." She inhaled a deep breath and slowly released it. "This is going to be great."

"Yes. I believe it will be." He released one of her hands to point at her. "All because of you."

"And you," she acknowledged.

"Well, maybe a little." He smirked as her face lit into a gorgeous smile.

"Thank you again, Bright, for everything."

"Hey, I couldn't have done it without your help or your faith in me."

"Yes, you could have. I just wish—"

"What?" he asked.

"I just wish you could be out here with me, instead of working in the kitchen."

His heart did the now familiar jump in his chest as she looked up at him, the lights about the room casting a sparkle to her eyes. "You know what?" he asked.

"What?"

"I wish I could be too, because I'm having a hard time walking away from you right now."

Her cheeks flushed as she turned her eyes away and he gently nudged her chin up so she'd look him in the eye once more. "I think you're the most beautiful woman I've ever seen, Mary Rutherford. And quite possibly the sweetest."

Her eyes sparkled at his words and she raised herself up on her toes. But before their lips could meet, a crash sounded from the kitchen. Embarrassed at her actions, Mary backed away as Bright inwardly berated the staff member who'd ruined the moment. Regretfully, he smoothed his thumb over her hand, "I better go check that out."

"Right." She nervously backed away, but he didn't relinquish his hold on her hand.

"Save that for me, will you?"

"What?"

"Whatever was about to happen."

She flushed and before she could respond, her mother was walking back into the room to hurry her towards the front entry. Bright dropped her hand and walked towards the kitchen.

« CHAPTER EIGHT »

Mary's face ached from smiling, her feet sore from the stiletto heels hidden beneath the heavy satin skirt she wore, and her brain tired from trying to remember names. However, she felt pleased with the party and the guests. Her father had established a wonderful team of employees at R&S, and all had been cheerful about the changes to the party invitations. Toys arrived by the bundle, and she'd walked by several groups of people as they munched and complimented on the food throughout the night. Bright's classic dishes were a hit, and she proudly bragged about his hard work to any eager listener.

Emily Higgins, soon to be Downs once again, walked up with a confident and slink stride, her manicured hand carrying what seemed to be her fourth champagne flute of the night. She beamed and gave Mary a light hug. "Mary, this party is wonderful! I couldn't have done it better myself." She pointed to a man over by the tree in the parlor who placed his gift alongside all the others. 'That's Stan, he's my number two, you just have to meet him. He's new. Stan!" she called, waving the man over. Stan, a new recruit for R&S Distribution, had a set of wide shoulders, narrow waist, and a strut that only Fabio could compete with. His smile, also alarmingly white, held a touch of ego that Mary knew she'd soon see on full display.

"Stan, this is Mary Rutherford."

His face slightly altered as he realized he was meeting the boss's daughter and only heir. He extended his hand. "Nice to meet you, Mary."

"Welcome to the R&S team," Mary greeted.

"Thank you. I've enjoyed getting to know everyone." His gaze lingered on Emily a touch longer than was polite before he forced a polite smile back to Mary.

"You are in acquisitions?" Mary asked.

"That I am. Under this magnificent lady's leadership." He mocked a bow towards Emily, who lightly held a hand to her heart as she laughed.

Mary, unsure how she felt about their flirtatious banter, listened as the two of them bounced ideas off one another while also trying to fill her in on all their successes from the year. Clearly, Emily knew Mary was potentially about to take over the family business. She gently rested a hand on Emily's arm. "If you'll excuse me." She offered an apologetic glance to Stan. "It was nice to meet you." She hurried off, exhausted by the banter. She ducked her way through the crowd towards the kitchen and slipped quietly inside to see Bright motioning several servers out the opposite door with replenished trays as he stood behind the counter mixing what looked to be another batch of dressing in a large metal bowl. He glanced up briefly to see who'd entered his domain and almost dropped his spoon in surprise. He recovered and answered two more questions from servers and pointed to various items that needed to make their way out the door. "You're in the wrong room, Ms. Rutherford." His deep voice had several heads turning and then scurrying about their tasks.

"I needed a break. Mind if I sit in here a spell."

"Only if you eat." He walked towards the far wall, where warming ovens boasted platefuls of

Christmas dinners already prepared. He pulled one out and slid it to a spot at the bar opposite him. "Eat."

"How do you know I haven't already?"

"I can tell."

She accepted the silverware from a passing server. "What's with the ready-made plates?"

"I figured the servers would get hungry throughout the evening, so I set us all some aside and they can eat in shifts."

His thoughtfulness caused her to pause with the fork halfway towards her mouth. "Are you serious?"

He looked up from his stirring. "Should I not have?"

"No. I mean, yes, well... it's supremely kind of you, Bright."

"Oh," He continued stirring and then poured the mixture into a foil pan and slid it into an oven, hitting buttons on a timer before handing the bowl to a maid at the sink. She washed with a speed Mary had only seen in top restaurants. "Well, we all have to eat or we'll be dead on our feet... like you."

"I'm just tired of talking to people."

"Then I'll take the hint." He smiled as he moved to walk towards another counter space to work.

Her hand shot out fast to land on top of his. "No. Please don't. That's not what I meant."

"I know." He winked as he crossed his arms. "So... how goes it out there?"

"Good. Everyone *loves* the food."

"That's what I like to hear."

"And I've met every single person it seems like."

"Which is good if you plan on taking over the company."

Her eyes widened as she shushed him. "No one is supposed to know."

He grimaced. "No one heard me. They're all too busy. So, have you made a decision?"

"Not yet. I have until tomorrow."

"Cuttin' it kind of close, aren't you, Rutherford?"

"There's still a lot to consider, *Smith*," she stressed.

He grinned at her sassy reply. "Well, I, much like your dad, can't wait to hear what you decide."

"You alright back here?" she asked.

"Surprisingly, yes."

"Good. Thank you, again. I think I will keep thanking you for the next year."

He laughed. "Thank me when the party is over. We'll see if I can make it without any mishaps."

"I have full confidence in you."

"Mary, what on Earth are you doing in here?" Her mother's voice drifted towards her in horror. "You are to be mingling with the guests."

"I just needed a short breather, Mom. I'm headed back out." Mary nudged her half-eaten plate towards Bright.

Molly eyed Bright for a moment before diverting her disapproving gaze towards Mary. "Well, your father is about to make his speech. We are to be in the parlor by the tree."

"I'm on my way." Mary stood, a hiss of pain escaping her lips as she adjusted to standing on her sore feet. "See you later."

"Good luck out there," Bright whispered, already clearing her plate and turning to his next task.

With dread, Mary followed her mother out of the room. She cast a quick glance back into the kitchen at Bright. He stood, two plates in his hands as he watched her leave. When their gazes met, she hesitated a brief moment before her mother tugged on her hand. "Wait." She pulled her hand away from her mother's. "Give me one more second." She hurried back into the kitchen and towards Bright, who'd already begun preparing the pan of dressing he'd planned to pop in the oven. He turned in surprise. "Come to the parlor at midnight. That's when everyone sings Christmas carols and ushers in Christmas."

"I don't know, Mary." He looked down at his once-white apron.

"Please. I'd like you to be there." The intensity of his eyes on her had her heart racing and skin heating. The stifling air around them was not only noticeable to Mary, but to other staff members in the room and her mother. Mary felt herself take a step closer to him, her feet floating as if they had a mind of their own.

Bright looked down at her, his usually smiling face serious, and his voice quiet. "I'll be there, Mary."

Relieved, she smiled. "Good. See you then, Bright." She hurried towards her mother and out the door.

::

The chaos of the kitchen had slowed to a crawl now that time had ticked by into the late hours of the night. He checked the clock on the wall and saw he had five minutes until midnight.

Several of the staff sat at the long counter eating their first meal of the evening with glee, as if the Christmas cheer outside the walls of the kitchen had slowly seeped inside the room to lighten the mood. He allowed them the moment of sitting and eating a warm meal, knowing if they were half as exhausted as he was, that they deserved it. He removed his apron and draped it on one of the bar stools. Several of the servers glanced up at him with curious expressions.

"I'm going to slip out a few minutes. Just keep an eye on the dessert trays out there."

They nodded obediently and went about their meals. He walked to the small bath off the kitchen and gave himself a once over. He looked a bit frayed around the edges, but he'd somehow kept his dark green sweater free of stains. He attempted to smooth his disheveled hair a bit before exiting and heading out to the party.

His eyes widened at the sight of all the people. Yes, he'd known the party would be crowded, but actually seeing the crowd was a bit overwhelming. *He'd cooked for all of these people?* The task almost seemed impossible to think about, but he'd done it. And at the thought of a job well done, the ache between his shoulder blades eased and he allowed himself to relax just a little. He walked towards the main parlor, the enormous tree a beacon for his weary feet, much like a lighthouse for a sea-tired sailor. Gifts puddled around the bottom, overflowed, and stacked upon one another. Clearly the toy drive had been a success. He spotted Mary standing near her parents by the base of the tree, a microphone stand in front of her father and mother as they waited for the countdown to midnight. After hours of mingling, she still looked stunning. Not a hair was out of place, her polished face glowing amidst the Christmas lights and sparkle of the room. He felt himself straighten to his full height when she spotted him, and he liked that her face split into a pleased smile, her eyes eager to see him as she waved him over. He pardoned his way through droves of people, Mary meeting him a few steps away from her parents. She grabbed his hands and squeezed them. "We did it," she whispered. "I've heard people talking all night about how this was the best party yet." Her eyes danced as she looked up at him in adoration. "Thank you, Bright. My parents want to give you a formal thank you." She tugged him towards her parents, her father spotting him and clearing his throat before tapping a knife to his champagne flute. The talking in the room ceased as he stepped up to the microphone.

"Another wonderful year at R&S Distribution." A round of applause swept the room. "I am thankful for each and every one of you. Not only have we increased our numbers for the year, but look at what all you have done tonight." He motioned towards the overflowing toy donations. "I want to give my daughter, Mary, the credit for such an idea. When she first pitched the idea to me, I wasn't so sure if we had enough time to pull it off, but in true R&S fashion, we rallied and came together and look at all the gifts for the children in our area. Thank you, Mary." More applause as Mary shyly waved her hand, her other hand still clutching Bright's.

"And a special thank you to Brighten Smith for catering tonight's event. I speak for all of us, Bright, when I say the food was beyond wonderful. Whether you aimed to or not, I believe you have just launched a catering business. At least once a year for us, anyway." He chuckled as several others did as well. Bright nodded his thanks as Mary's hand tightened on his for a moment. Her father continued sharing stories from the work year, giving several employees their moment of glory from the boss as he shined attention on their accomplishments. Bright barely heard a word. All he could think about was Mary standing next to him. She'd removed her hand from his and linked her arm through his elbow instead. He was underdressed standing next to her, but he still felt like a million dollars. Her father tapped the microphone, "Testing. Testing." He mimicked a few vocal warmups to a pleased crowd before launching into Jingle Bells, the string quartet accommodating his choice in music. Everyone began singing. He placed his hand over the one Mary'd placed in his arm. She looked at him and her brows furrowed at his slowly slipping away. "Where are you going?" she asked.

"I need to get back to clean up in the kitchens, if I'm ever to wrap it up back there."

Disappointment wrinkled her brow. "Surely you have a few more minutes."

He caught her mother's pointed gaze over Mary's shoulder, her aggravation at her daughter's distracted behavior not going unnoticed. Bright relinquished himself from Mary. "Sorry. I'll try to touch base with you before I leave."

He felt like a coward leaving her there, but he didn't want to muddy the waters with her mother. Mary had a job to do for the night, and so did he. He was hired to cater, and he was technically still on the clock. No matter how badly he wished to continue mingling with Mary, his role was that of a hired employee for the night, not as a friend. And he hoped that by sticking to those guidelines, he'd impress the Rutherfords enough that they might consider him good enough for their daughter down the road.

« CHAPTER NINE »

Tired, worn out, exhausted, weary, and fatigued. No matter which way she put it, that's how Mary felt on Christmas morning. Just barely Christmas morning, she reminded herself. The clock struck two and she found herself standing in front of the gorgeous tree crowded by all the presents, sipping the last of a champagne flute, and basking in the warmth that came from an earned success. She'd made up her mind about her dad's offer. She'd take the position at R&S. If a group of people could come together to bring this many Christmas wishes to fruition, then she could only imagine what they could do as a company working together. Her father knew every single person in the room the night before. He greeted them by name, introduced them to her, spoke of their position in the company, whether it was a mailman, a secretary, or his management team, and praised them for at least one positive contribution they'd brought to the company for the year. *True leadership*, she thought, and she sorted through faces and names so that once she did step into her dad's shoes, she could be just as intentional. No wonder so many people liked working for R&S. Her dad had created a family environment. Yes, she thought it somewhat ironic, since they'd never experienced much of a family-oriented homelife, but the sweetness was there. From a young age, her father had worked at the distribution center. It was no surprise he'd consider them all family. And now she hoped to do the same. Sighing, she reached beneath the hem of her skirt and removed her high heels. "Freedom," she whispered, as she tossed them aside.

A throat cleared and had her startling before she realized it was Bright. He looked as she felt, only she could swear that despite his tired expression, he was the most attractive man she'd ever laid eyes on.

"Isn't it past your curfew, Ms. Rutherford?"

She grinned. "Absolutely. Though technically, I'm already at home. I thought you'd left already. I checked the kitchens a while ago."

"I was in the freezer for a bit, organizing the remaining food. I figured you guys could eat it, donate it, or toss it. I just didn't want to make that decision for you. Everything's labeled."

"You're a superstar, Brighten Smith." Mary walked over to a cocktail table and grabbed another flute of champagne and walked it over to him. "Cheers," she toasted and clinked her glass to his.

He took a long sip and followed her gaze to the tree. "You did it. You pulled off the best Christmas extravaganza in ages."

Mary giggled softly as she set her glass aside. "Only with your help. Oh, I've something for you."

His brows rose. "Me?"

"Yep." She grinned and motioned him towards the base of the tree. "It's Christmas morning, Bright. Have a seat at the base of the tree. Isn't that what normal families do when opening gifts?"

He laughed. "I suppose so." He eased to the soft rug that barely peeked out from beneath all the toy gifts and sat. "Wow." He stretched his legs. "I think this is the first time I've sat in hours. I'm stiff legged."

She walked over and sat on her haunches, her full skirt spread around her in a circle of satiny darkness. Reaching into the tree branches, towards the back of the tree, she removed a small box wrapped in glittery blue paper. "Open it," she urged him as he looked at her speechless. "Go on." She nudged his shoulder, "Don't leave me in suspense."

"But you already know what it is."

She laughed. "True, but I want to see what you think about it. No pressure." She held her hands out in front of her as if to ward off any stress her words may have caused.

"Alright." Bright pulled the ribbon off the small package and tore the paper. He opened the small box and paused.

"Like it?" Her hands were clasped in her lap and she prayed he found the gift fun. Though it was nowhere near enough to repay him for all his help, she hoped that it was a token of how much she personally appreciated and thought about him.

A slow smile spread over his face. "Mary, Mary, Mary." He shook his head and then laughed. "A Millennium Falcon ornament?"

She nervously bit her lip.

"I *love* it! This is awesome! Where did you find this?"

"Mr. Destin helped me," she admitted. "I saw it in a catalog and just knew I had to get it for you. I know it's not much, considering what all you've done over the last few weeks."

"Which I was payed for," he pointed out.

"Right, but... well... I wanted to get you something myself."

He let the ornament dangle from his finger and grinned. "I think this is one of the best presents I've ever received." He reached over and squeezed her hand. "Thank you."

"You're welcome." She watched as he placed it gently back into the small box and began to rise.

"I'm beat. If I'm to show up at Grace's house full of Christmas cheer in a few hours, I need to catch at least a couple of hours of sleep." He helped Mary to her feet. "I see you've discarded the heels."

"Finally." She closed her eyes as she sighed with deep pleasure.

Chuckling, he lightly brushed a thumb down her cheek. Her eyes popped open at the contact and he stood closer to her than he had before. "I think I will always remember the way you look tonight, right now, in front of the tree. You're radiant, Mary Rutherford." His voice quieted as his eyes lingered on hers, his hand gently cupping her cheek. She leaned into his touch and felt him slowly pull her towards him.

Her hand pressed against his chest as his free arm slid around her waist to hold her against him. "May I?" he asked.

She didn't answer, but instead, closed the distance between them by pressing her lips against his. Her stomach dropped to her toes and then soared back up again in a rolling wave. Warmth radiated through her bones and relaxed her muscles, leaving her soft and relaxed in his embrace. His kiss sent thrills down her spine and into her nervous fingers as they slid around his neck and up into his hair. The kiss deepened and she felt like the rug beneath her feet was a cloud, floating higher and higher. When he eased away, he rested his forehead against hers. "I should go."

Breathless, Mary nodded in silence, her heart on a rampage. Her hands rested over his chest and she felt the same thing happening to him. It pleased her to know she could make him feel the same way she did.

"Can I see you later today?" he asked.

Again, she wordlessly nodded, not escaping the close proximity of him. His hands slid up and down her exposed arms and she felt goose flesh rise upon her skin despite the wave of warmth rushing through her.

He kissed her forehead. "Merry Christmas, Mary." His hands slid down her arms and to her hands.

"Merry Christmas, Bright."

He hesitated a moment longer, the brightness of a flash breaking their trance. Rowan Rutherford stood in the doorway. "I hope you don't mind," he cheerfully announced. "The lighting was just too perfect."

"I thought you were in bed, Dad." Embarrassment stained Mary's cheeks as she reluctantly released Bright's hands.

"On my way up actually." Rowan stepped further into the room. "I believe, Mr. Smith, that you are the best caterer we've ever hired."

"Thank you, sir." Bright accepted his handshake.

"Mary, I hope you will get some rest this morning."

"I plan to, Dad."

"Good. Well, I will leave you two young people to it. This old man is tired." He offered a brief smile before walking back towards the door.

"Oh, Dad." Mary called after him and had him turning with a tired smile. "Yes. My answer is yes."

He nodded, a pleased and proud expression lighting his eyes. "Wonderful news this morning, Mary. Indeed, a wonderful Christmas gift. We will talk more later. Rest, you two." He called towards them as he walked up the winding staircase towards his bedroom.

"You're staying?" Bright asked.

"Yes. Well, I plan to come back, I should say. I have to go back to Landisburg to tie up loose ends, but it was clear to me last night that my place is here at R&S."

"Wow." Bright studied her a moment longer before pulling her into a tight hug. "I think the gifts just keep on coming. Prepare to be annoyed by me, Mary Rutherford, because you're going to see my face more often."

"I was hoping you'd say that." Mary grinned up at him before he planted another firm kiss on her lips. He quickly nudged her away. "Okay, I need to go now, or I'll never leave."

She giggled as he hurried towards the door, jingling his keyring on his finger. "I'll call you or see you, one of the two at some point today."

"Can't wait. Please tell Nonnie and your family Merry Christmas for me."

Their eyes met across the room. "I will. Good morning, Mary." He winked as he stepped out of the room, leaving her again, basking in the subtle glow of twinkling lights.

::

"I had twenty bucks on you ruining at least one dish last night." Grace, disappointed at the loss of some cash, but pleased to see her brother on time and ready for the family's Christmas day events, smirked up at him as she sat rubbing her rotund belly.

"Oh, now Grace," Nonnie waved a dish towel her way as she removed the roasted turkey from the oven and placed it on the counter. "Bright had everything under control, I'm sure. And the evening went swimmingly, I have no doubt."

"Thanks, Nonnie." Bright kissed her cheek as he stepped around her to wash his hands at the sink.

"And Mary," Nonnie continued. "How's Mary after last night?"

"Good. She's decided to stay in Ransforth and take over R&S Distribution."

His words caused Nonnie's hands to still and Grace paused with her mug of hot cocoa halfway to her lips.

He caught their dumbfounded expressions. "What?"

"Did she really?" Nonnie asked.

"Yes. She gave her answer to her dad this morning right in front of me."

Grace hid her smile as she took a sip of her drink.

"I'm surprised she said yes," Nonnie admitted.

"I'm not," Bright continued. "You should have seen her last night, Nonnie. She was radiant. She attempted to meet every single person there while also checking in on me and handling the party issues as well."

"Sounds like a pretty powerful woman." Grace leaned back in her chair on a sigh.

"She is." Bright smiled. "Powerful and kind, which is a rare combination."

"That she is." Nonnie reached for the mashed potatoes and gave them a fresh pat of butter and a stir. "And will she be joining us today?" Her voice held a touch of prying grandmother mixed with nonchalance. Grace nibbled her bottom lip to keep from laughing at their grandmother's curiosity and matchmaking hopes.

"No." Bright, oblivious towards his grandmother's prying, set about filling cups with ice and tea. "If she's smart, she'll sleep into next week. But I plan to meet up with her later today at some point."

"That's good." Nonnie flashed a quick glance towards Grace. "Did you get her a Christmas gift?"

"No." Bright shook his head. "But she did get me one, which was surprising."

"She got you a gift?" Grace asked. "What was it?"

"An ornament."

Nonnie placed a hand over her heart. "That's darling."

"I think the biggest gift will be her moving here though," Bright confessed. "I will admit, I'm pretty happy about her decision."

"Is this Mary someone you could see dating in the future?" Grace asked plainly.

Bright flushed as he glanced up at their two curious faces.

"Well, that answers that." Grace grinned into her cup.

"I didn't say anything."

"You didn't have to, Bright. Your face says it all. You like her."

"Well, yeah. She's great."

"Just great?" Nonnie asked.

"Alright, now I see what you two are doing." He walked a few glasses towards the dining room and set them at place settings.

"Hey, you're the one that blushed," Grace called out.

He laughed as he walked back into the room. "Okay then, I'll come clean. I *do* like Mary. And I will even go as far as to confess to you two nosey ladies that I kissed her just this morning."

Nonnie's hands stilled as Grace's jaw dropped in surprise.

"That's right," Bright added. "In front of the Christmas tree, no less. So you two can keep your matchmaking wheels on halt, because I'm doing this my way and my own speed."

"Brighten, Brighten, Brighten..." Nonnie gently rested a hand on his arm.

"Don't worry, Nonnie. I'll be kind to her."

"Oh, I know you will, sweetie."

"I know she's important to you. And over the last several weeks, well, she's become important to me too."

"I'm glad." Her eyes misted over.

He looked over at his sister. "Don't try to run her off, either."

"Now why would I do that?" Grace spread her hands open on the table. "Oh, that's right, because no one liked your last girlfriend and thought you were a fool for moving to California. Got it."

He frowned as she chortled. "Bright, from what Nonnie's told me about Mary, and seeing you two interacting on the parade float, I'd say you are the one that needs to be cautious."

"Why's that?"

"Because that woman has you wrapped around her finger."

"Is that a bad thing?"

"Depends on the woman."

"Mary isn't like other women. She's sweet, shy, considerate, intelligent, and—"

"Whoa, Romeo." Grace held up her hand to stop him. "I don't doubt that. I just know what I saw was more than just a 'date here and there' vibe. If you and Mary progress, I see wedding bells in the near future."

"Grace," Nonnie warned.

"I'm calling it now."

"And if that happens," Bright interrupted. "I'd count myself the luckiest man alive."

Nonnie softly gasped. "Bright." Her breathless tone had his shoulders straighten.

"It's true. I know what Mary means to me. I know that if what I feel for her now grows, it will lead to just what Grace said. I'm also not afraid of that. California was wrong for me. The 'woman that shall not be named' was all wrong for me. Mary... well, she's not like that."

"Then I wish you luck." Grace toasted her mug towards him. "And I better meet her soon."

"You will. Everyone will." Bright walked into Grace's living room to find it empty, the kids already bundled up and outside playing with their new toys in the backyard. He sat, sipping his glass of tea and staring at the colorful twinkling lights on Grace's tree. He could still picture Mary in her billowing black skirt, sleek hair, and sequined top from the night before. Each time he did, his heart did a funny flip. *Was he crazy? Was it too soon to play his hand and hope that the deck was in his favor? Did Mary feel the same way he did?* He thought she might, especially after their kiss. But she would have a lot on her plate here soon. Would she want to start a relationship in the midst of all her life changes? His phone buzzed in his pocket. Mary's name lit across the screen and he swiped his thumb to answer. "I was just thinking about you. Have you slept the day away?"

He could hear the smile in her voice. "No, actually. I woke up to have amazing leftovers for lunch. Someone left them so neatly labeled in the freezer. I am now slipping on my shoes to make my gift deliveries."

"Oh? And where all are you going?"

"I'm headed over to one of the shelters with some of the toy gifts."

"You're doing that today?"

"It's Christmas." Her simple response had him baffled by her generosity once again.

"You should swing by Grace's on your way home. We will be about ready to eat by then. You should join us."

"Oh, I don't want to intrude on family time. Besides, my dad wanted to talk to me this evening about the job, so I'll probably be tied up with that for a bit. But—" She trailed off.

"But?"

"What does Christmas day look like for you *after* your big meal?"

Bright leaned back in the cushioned chair and relaxed. "Well, it looks like me meeting a beautiful woman under the gazebo downtown for some hot chocolate and cookies, I believe."

"Oh does it?" Her soft lilted laughter had his pulse drumming. "She must be a lovely woman to receive such attention."

"She is. You should meet her. Want to meet us there?" he teased.

"I think I'd like that. What time?"

"Eight."

"I'll be there," Mary replied. "And Bright?"

"Yes?"

A long pause held over the line before she finally said, "I can't wait to see you."

He hung up and did a silent celebratory fist pump in the air.

"Did I seriously just witness that?" Grace asked on a laugh.

Bright grinned. "I'm meeting Mary later."

"So I heard." Grace rested a hand over his shoulder. "Mary and Bright... as if that couldn't get any cuter for Christmas." She gave him one last encouraging pat before waddling back into the kitchen.

« CHAPTER TEN »

February

The gazebo was no longer lit with twinkling Christmas lights. Though some of the snow remained, the holidays had passed into an uproarious new year and Mary drove the familiar path into Ransforth from Landisburg. It was official. She started work at her father's, nay, *her* company today. She pulled into the front parking spot outside of Nonnie's bakery and hurried inside. During the holidays, her entrance would have set off a chorus of Christmas carols, but now, it had its familiar chime. Nonnie walked into the room, wiping her hands on a dish towel. She brightened at the sight of Mary. "How's my girl?"

"A bit nervous," Mary admitted. "I thought I might need a Nonnie cookie to help ease the nerves."

"Hmm... I think I have just the thing." Nonnie walked towards the display counter and opened a small bakery box and began placing an array of cookies inside it. "For sharing."

"Thank you."

"So how is the move coming along?"

"Officially handed over my keys this morning. I am now a full-time resident of Ransforth starting today."

"And have you told Bright?"

"Yes." Mary beamed at the thought of Brighten Smith, the man who'd so quickly swept into her life and become more than just a high school memory.

"We plan to celebrate this evening."

"Wonderful." Nonnie handed her the box. "You go get 'em, Mary Rutherford."

She leaned over the counter and gave Nonnie an embrace. "What I would do without your faith in me, Nonnie? I'll never know."

"And you won't have to." Nonnie brushed a hand over Mary's hair. "Now go to your new adventure."

Mary hurried out the door, her head bent low against the cold and ran smack into a firm chest.

"Easy there." Bright's voice had her head popping up, and before she could smile, his lips were on hers. "Last minute nerves?"

Her eyes were still closed from his kiss. "Not anymore." She opened her eyes to find his shining face. "I needed that."

"Me too. I'm glad to see you made it in early this morning."

"I couldn't sleep a wink, so when the clock hit five, I was already dressed and on my way. What are your plans for the day?"

"I've got some design projects I need to knock out for a client, but after that I will be here with Nonnie."

"Until lunch time." Mary waved a hand over herself. "Where you'll meet me."

"Oh, are we doing that today?"

"Yes, we are." She grinned as she gave him one last kiss before walking towards her car and opened the driver's side door.

Bright held it open for her. "I could get used to this."

Mary slid into her seat and looked up at him. "Me too."

"I'll see you at lunch, Ms. Rutherford." He shut her door and she offered one final wave before driving the short distance to the distribution center.

Her father awaited her, keeping warm in his car until she pulled up next to him. They'd agreed to come to the office early so as to get her settled in.

"Right on time." He eased out of his car and Mary held up the box from Nonnie.

"And I come bearing gifts."

"Delightful ones at that." Rowan motioned for her to follow him inside, the security officer at the door alert and welcoming. "Andrew," Rowan greeted.

Mary held open the box for Andrew to have first pick of the cookies and he snatched a chocolate chip. "Thank you, Ms. Rutherford."

"Happy Monday, Andrew." She followed her father into the elevator.

"You seem cheerful for a Monday."

"It's the start of a new chapter, Dad."

"That it is."

"I look forward to it."

"As do I. Though I must say, I had the most intriguing phone call this morning."

"Oh?"

"Yes. It would seem your Mr. Smith would like to meet me at ten this morning. Something about rebranding."

"Ah. Well, he is a graphic designer, maybe he has some ideas for R&S to update some signage or something."

"Possibly." Rowan slyly smiled as he opened the door to what would now be Mary's office right next door to his. "Alright, let's get started."

::

At ten o clock, Bright sat in the small coffee shop awaiting Rowan Rutherford. When he saw the man's luxury sedan pull into the parking lot, his nerves started jumping. He ordered himself to keep his cool, to appear confident, self-assured. This was the pitch of his life.

Rowan entered and removed his hat and scarf on the way to the table, signaling to the waitress for a cup of warm brew. When he sat, he held up his hand and waited until his coffee was delivered to the table before speaking.

"Mr. Rutherford, thank you for meeting with me."

"It's a pleasure, Brighten. But let us just toss away the pretense of a sales pitch. You want to marry my daughter, don't you?"

Bright choked on his coffee as Rowan Rutherford sat across from him with a stern and serious face. "Wow, um... sir. I—"

Slowly, the façade slipped away and Rowan beamed. "I think it a marvelous idea."

Bright's brows shot into his hairline. "You do?"

"Of course I do. I knew it the moment I snapped your photo by the Christmas tree." He took a long sip of his coffee and set the cup onto its saucer.

"You have no objections?"

"Why would I? You are a kind, generous, hardworking young man who is crazy about my daughter."

"I just thought—"

"If you're worried whether or not I think it too soon, I will admit I was concerned at first. But upon further reflection, I realized that Molly will not settle for Mary having a mediocre wedding and therefore the planning will take months, which in turn will prolong the engagement for quite some time. The wedding will not be a rushed affair, you see, and the time frame of your courtship is now inconsequential."

Bright only stared as Mary's father continued. "Furthermore, you come from a respectable family that will embrace Mary for who she is and not for what she's worth. That is important."

"Yes sir." Bright, still dumb struck, could think of nothing else to say in response.

"And she loves you." Rowan held up his hands. "Isn't that the simplest of answers one needs to make such a call?"

"She does?" Bright asked and then shook his head. "Well, I mean, I hope she does. I love her." He was fumbling. Crashing. Fast.

Mr. Rutherford nodded. "Of course she does. One only has to be around her five minutes to see she is in love with someone. And since you are the only gentleman in her life, naturally that means with you."

"Okay..."

"Have I completely fried your brain?" Rowan paused and a look of nervous jitters crossed his features. "Oh dear, did I misread this? Are you in fact here for an actual business proposal for R&S and not Mary? Oh feathers," he mumbled. "I've completely botched things, haven't I?"

"No." Bright leaned back in his chair. "Not at all. I mean..." He inhaled a deep breath. "Alright, I'm just going to lay everything out onto the table since you've been kind enough to do the same."

"Go on." Rowan waited, his hands fiddling with what was probably his tenth cup of coffee for the morning.

"I do love Mary," Bright confessed. "Very much. I haven't told her yet, though. I plan to today. And yes, I did wish to ask for your blessing on moving forward with your daughter. Though I hadn't planned on proposing today, I just wanted you to know my intentions."

"I see."

Bright studied him a moment. "I *do* want to propose to her though... for the record."

Rowan smiled. "I should hope so, not only because of my spiel, but because, as you say, you love her and she loves you."

They sat silent a moment.

"Do you really think she'd say yes if I asked today?"

Mr. Rutherford nodded. "I do." He stood to his feet and slipped back into his trench coat. "Think on it, Brighten. Whatever you decide, you have my full blessing. Mary is… well, she's dear to me, though I didn't always show or tell her that over the years. I should like for her to find someone who treats her with an overwhelming amount of love. I wish for her to be cherished. I think, young man, that you could be that someone." He tapped his knuckles on the table. "Good day."

Bright stared after him in shock. Rowan Rutherford had just given him the blessing to marry his daughter as if he'd thought of the idea himself. Flattered he held Bright in such esteem, he also feared Mary might be more hesitant to the idea than her father. Perhaps, his first move would be to just share his feelings. *Best not to overwhelm her*, he thought. Or himself.

::

It wasn't Valentine's Day, she *did* know that much, so when she pulled up to see the gazebo lit up with twinkle lights sparkling against the gray sky, a small table dressed in white linens and flowers resting on a chair, Mary had to blink a few times to make sure she was really seeing Bright stand there with a large carafe of hot chocolate for just a regular lunch date. His text to meet him at the center of the town square wasn't abnormal. They'd fit in walks around town several times over the last couple of months. But lunch? "What is all this?" She beamed as she climbed the steps and tiptoed to give him a kiss on the lips on her way to a chair. He hurried over and pulled out one of the two chairs and waited for her to sit and handed her the bouquet of flowers. "Bright, this is quite the elaborate set up for hot chocolate and lunch. Are we celebrating something?"

"Your first day on the job."

"Which isn't over yet," she pointed out.

"Oh, that's right. I guess we should celebrate something else then. How about how much I love you?"

Mary's brows shot up. "You what?"

He laughed. "Thought that might get your attention." He reached across the table for her hand. "I love you, Mary Rutherford."

Her eyes never left his as he kissed her hand. "And though I want to scream it from the rooftops and bend down on one knee and ask you to be my wife, I don't want to freak you out just yet."

She released a relieved breath as her heart pounded in her chest. "Bright, I—"

"I spoke with your dad earlier this morning about my intentions and he's given me his full blessing."

"You spoke to my dad?" Stunned, she felt her skin warm at the thought he'd taken the time to do such a sweet gesture.

"I did. Now, like I said, I'm not proposing today, but Mary, I do want you to know that I *do* plan to one day. I want our relationship to continue to grow and mature, because I love you. Have I said that already?"

"Are you going to let me say anything?" she asked on a laugh, cutting off his nervous fumbling.

He leaned back in his chair, releasing her hand and nodded, though she still saw his right leg bouncing beneath the table. His cheerful attitude was slipping into apprehension at her delayed response.

"Bright," She walked over and sat on his lap, her left arm draped around his shoulders. "I love you too."

He looked up at her announcement and a slow smile spread over his face. "You do?"

"Very much." She choked on the last word as tears threatened to fall.

He exhaled a long breath. "*That* is definitely news worth celebrating."

She chuckled softly as she kissed his lips. "And I don't want to steal your thunder, but—"

"But what?" His dark eyes held the familiar kindness, understanding, and charm they always did as she lightly kissed his lips again for courage.

"Will you marry *me*?" she asked.

"Mary, I told you I wanted to marry you. What makes you think I don't want to?"

"No, Bright, will you?"

"Again, I told you I wanted to." His confusion had her laughing, and she smoothed a finger over his wrinkled forehead.

"Bright!" She cupped his face in her hands. "I'm asking you right *now*."

His face paled a moment as he realized the gravity of her question and his mistake in assuming she meant later like he'd planned. "You want to marry me, *now*?"

"If you'll have me." She giggled as he leapt to his feet, bringing her with him, carrying her in his arms and spinning around in circles.

"Yes. Yes!" He set her to her feet and kissed her firmly on the lips. "I thought you might think it was too soon, even though your dad assured me it wasn't. So, I played it safe."

She held a finger to his lips and he stopped talking. "Just kiss me, Bright."

"Gladly." He cupped her cheek in his hand and kissed her, melting away her insecurities at asking him such a question. "So, when should we set the date?" he asked, his eagerness making her smile brighten even further.

"I was thinking Christmas."

He swung her around once more. "Perfect. May our Christmas be Mary and Bright, then."

"Exactly what I was thinking." Mary rested her forehead against his as she basked in his presence. How had it been less than a few months ago that she lived life without him? "I love you, Brighten Smith."

Bright tucked her hair behind her ear and brushed his thumb over the curve of her cheek. "And I you, Mary Rutherford.

TWO YEARS LATER

Rowan Rutherford reached for his wife's hand as they climbed down the stairs on Christmas morning. Though they were still a bit bleary eyed from the company Christmas party the night before, this Christmas morning required their early participation in front of the Christmas tree. They walked into the parlor to find Brighten Smith, their daughter's husband, cradling his one-year-old daughter in his arms and showing her the bright twinkling lights on the tree.

"How's our little princess this morning?" Rowan walked forward and scooped the little girl from Bright's arms.

"Great. Sybil is in love with all the lights."

Molly Rutherford brushed her finger down the girl's soft cheek. "It amazes me how much she looks like Mary at this age."

Sybil smiled and gave a small squeal towards her grandmother and Molly cooed. "Oh, darlin', yes, come to Gran." She stole the girl from her husband and walked her over to the grand windows that overlooked the wide front lawn covered in snow.

"And Mary?" Rowan asked.

"She was gathering a tray of goodies to set up in here."

"And here they are," Mary's voice rang out as she wheeled a small cart with coffee and cookies. "Merry Christmas, Dad."

Rowan gave her a small hug.

"Where's Mom?"

Rowan pointed across the room. "Showing Sybil the fresh snow."

Molly turned and walked over. "Oh, how wonderful, Mary!" She picked up a small piece of gingerbread and let Sybil sniff it before the little girl grabbed it with slimy drool covered fingers and shoved it in her mouth with much enthusiasm.

"That's my girl." Bright grinned as her eyes lit up at his voice and she danced and wiggled in Molly's embrace, reaching out towards him. He grabbed her before she could lunge from her grandmother's arms.

"I think this is one of the most wonderful Christmas mornings." Molly held a hand to her heart as she watched her granddaughter devour the rest of the gingerbread. "Precious girl." She brushed a hand over Sybil's downy hair.

"Present time," Mary announced and walked over towards the small stack of gifts that rested under the tree. She handed one to her mother and father and one to Bright.

Bright set Sybil in front of her own packages to start tugging on wrapping paper and tissue paper. He watched as Rowan and Molly opened their gift, both pausing over the ornament Mary had gifted them. They didn't look up. Molly placed a hand over her mouth as Rowan sat in stunned silence.

Bright eyed Mary curiously as she motioned for him to open his. He tugged the ribbon away and paused when the ornament, a ceramic white circle with two blue baby footprints rested inside. He looked up at Mary and she beamed and nodded. "We're having another baby?" He hopped to his feet as Rowan and Molly looked up at the same time. He swooped Mary into his arms and spun her around. He set her to rights and hugged her tightly. "We have to call Nonnie."

"Oh, she should be opening her gift right about now." As Mary stated that, the phone began to ring.

"Mary, Mary, Mary." Molly stepped forward and hugged her closely. "Such a Merry Christmas." She pulled away slightly to fluff the ends of Mary's hair, her eyes softening and taking on a serious expression. "Thank you for making our Christmas so special. I'm sorry we didn't do the same for you over the years."

"Consider it a fresh start, Mom... I mean, Gran."

Sybil made the hard 'G' sound as she took a few stumbling steps towards Molly. Molly, enraptured by her granddaughter, scooped her up and hugged her tight. "I adore you. All of you." Molly hugged Mary once more before walking towards Bright and giving him a celebratory hug as cheers could be heard over the speaker of the phone.

Mary sat on the armrest of one of the chairs snuggled around the fireplace and watched as her family celebrated not only the holiday but the good news of their baby boy. Life in Ransforth had been a change over the last couple of years. She'd stepped into her father's shoes at R&S Distribution. She'd moved to Ransforth permanently. She'd married Brighten Smith, the amazing man in front of her showering their daughter with love and attention. And she'd gained the love of the entire Smith family, who'd be arriving in an hour or so to celebrate with the Rutherfords. She tried to memorize the moment, the family, the gifts, the tree. She still remembered the Christmas three years ago when she and Bright tackled the R&S party together and sat in awe of the twinkling lights and how that Christmas brought about this special one. She felt his hand at the small of her back and the light kiss to the top of her hair as Bright came and stood beside her, both watching her parents sitting on the floor acting goofy and playing with Sybil and her new toys. Content, she sighed happily.

"Merry Christmas, Mary," Bright whispered.

She glanced up into his loving gaze. "Merry Christmas, Bright."

Other Titles by Katharine E. Hamilton

INTRODUCING THE FAMILY

THE SIBLINGS O'RIFCAN SERIES   KATHARINE E. HAMILTON

The Complete Siblings O'Rifcan Series Available in Paperback, Ebook, and Audiobook

Claron

Riley

Layla

Chloe

Murphy

All titles in The Lighthearted Collection
Available in Paperback, Ebook, and
Audiobook

Chicago's Best

Montgomery House

Beautiful Fury

McCarthy Road

Check out the Epic Fantasy Adventure Available in Paperback, Ebook, and Audiobook

UTHENFADING LANDS

The Unfading Lands, Part One in The Unfading Lands Series

Darkness Divided, Part Two in The Unfading Lands Series

Redemption Rising, Part Three in The Unfading Lands Series

Subscribe to Katharine's Newsletter for news on upcoming releases and events!
https://www.katharinehamilton.com/subscribe.html

Find out more about Katharine and her works at:
www.katharinehamilton.com

Social Media is a great way to connect with Katharine. Check her out on the following:

Facebook: Katharine E. Hamilton
https://www.facebook.com/Katharine-E-Hamilton-282475125097433/

Twitter: @AuthorKatharine
Instagram: @AuthorKatharine

Contact Katharine:
khamiltonauthor@gmail.com

ABOUT THE AUTHOR

Katharine E. Hamilton began writing in 2008 and published her first children's book, <u>The Adventurous Life of Laura Bell</u> in 2009. She would go on to write and illustrate two more children's books, <u>Susie At Your Service</u> and <u>Sissy and Kat</u> between 2010-2013.

Though writing for children was fun, Katharine moved into Adult Fiction in 2015 with her release of <u>The Unfading Lands</u>, a clean, epic fantasy that landed in Amazon's Hot 100 New Releases on its fourth day of publication, reached #72 in the Top 100 in Epic Fantasy, and hit the Top 10,000 Best Sellers on all of Amazon in its first week. It has been listed as a Top 100 Indie Read for 2015 and a nominee for a Best Indie Book Award for 2016. The series did not stop there. <u>Darkness Divided: Part Two of The Unfading Land Series</u>, released in October of 2015 and claimed a spot in the Top 100 of its genre. <u>Redemption Rising: Part Three of The Unfading Lands Series</u> released in April 2016 and claimed a nomination for the Summer Indie Book Awards.

Though comfortable in the fantasy genre, Katharine decided to venture towards romance in 2017 and released the first novel in a collection of sweet, clean and wholesome romances: The Lighthearted Collection. <u>Chicago's Best</u> reached best seller status in its first week of publication and rested comfortably in the Top 100 for Amazon for three steady weeks, claimed a Reader's Choice Award, a TopShelf Indie Book Award, and ended up a finalist in the American Book Festival's Best Book Awards for 2017. <u>Montgomery House</u>, the second in the collection, released in August of 2017 and rested comfortably alongside its predecessor, claiming a Reader's Choice Award, and becoming Katharine's best-selling novel up to that point. Both were released in audiobook format in late 2017 and early 2018. <u>Beautiful Fury</u> is the third novel released in the collection and has claimed a Reader's Choice Award and a gold medal in the Authorsdb Best Cover competition. It has also been released in audiobook format with narrator Chelsea Carpenter lending her talents to bring it to life. Katharine and Chelsea have partnered on an ongoing project for creating audiobook marketing methods for fellow authors and narrators, all of which will eventually be published as a resource tool for others.

In August of 2018, Katharine brought to life a new clean contemporary romance series of a loving family based in Ireland. The Siblings O'Rifcan Series kicked off in August with <u>Claron</u>. <u>Claron</u> climbed to the Top 1000 of the entire Amazon store and has reached the Top 100 of the Clean and Wholesome genre a total of 11 times. He is Katharine's bestselling book thus far and lends to the success of the following books in the series: <u>Riley</u>, <u>Layla</u>, <u>Chloe</u>, and <u>Murphy,</u> each book earning their place in the Top 100 of their genre and Hot 100 New Releases. <u>Claron</u> was featured in Amazon's Prime Reading program March – June 2019. The series is also available in audiobook format with the voice talents of Alex Black.

A Love For All Seasons, a Sweet Contemporary Romance Series launched in July of 2019 with Summer's Catch, followed by Autumn's Fall in October. Winter's Call and Spring's Hope scheduled for 2021 release dates. The series follows a wonderful group of friends from Friday Harbor, Washington.

Taking into account her personal life of living on ranches, Katharine launched The Brother's of Hastings Ranch Series in 2020, the series following the life of seven brothers on a ranch in west Texas. Book One, Graham, has been an Amazon Best Seller four times since his debut.

Katharine has contributed to charitable Indie Anthologies as well as helped other aspiring writers journey their way through the publication process. She manages an online training course that walks fellow self-publishing and independently publishing writers through the publishing process as well as how to market their books.

She is a member of Women Fiction Writers of America, Texas Authors, IASD, and the American Christian Fiction Writers. She loves everything to do with writing and loves that she is able to continue sharing heartwarming stories to a wide array of readers.

Katharine graduated from Texas A&M University with a bachelor's degree in History. She lives on a ranch in south Texas with her husband Brad, sons Everett, and West, and their two dogs, Tulip and Paws.

Made in the USA
Middletown, DE
09 November 2020